Darling
NIKKI

Dear Reader:

Darling Nikki, the same title as the popular Prince hit from *Purple Rain*, includes the color purple interspersed throughout this tale about a female vixen involved in a love triangle. We follow Nikki Johnson as she deals with the drama of an ex-husband; a son whose girlfriend becomes pregnant; and a mother who reappears after a twenty-year absence. Mix in murder and the unfolding of dark secrets revealed, and you have a haunting thriller that keeps you surprised until the end.

I am pleased to introduce E.V. Adams and her debut novel, which is sure to create a buzz.

As always, thanks for the support shown to the Strebor Books family. We appreciate the love. For more information on our titles, please visit www.zanestore.com and you can find me on my personal website: www.eroticanoir.com. You can also join my online social network at www.planetzane.org.

Blessings,

Zane

Zane
Publisher
Strebor Books International
www.simonandschuster.com

ZANE PRESENTS

Darling NIKKI

E.V. ADAMS

SBI
STREBOR BOOKS
NEW YORK LONDON TORONTO SYDNEY

SB|
Strebor Books
P.O. Box 6505
Largo, MD 20792
http://www.streborbooks.com

© 2012 by E.V. Adams

ISBN 978-1-59309-394-5
ISBN 978-1-4516-4525-5 (e-book)
LCCN 2011938318

First Strebor Books trade paperback edition February 2012

Cover design: www.mariondesigns.com
Cover photograph: © Keith Saunders/Marion Designs

10 9 8 7 6 5 4 3 2 1

Manufactured in the United States of America

For information regarding special discounts for bulk purchases,
please contact Simon & Schuster Special Sales at 1-866-506-1949
or business@simonandschuster.com

The Simon & Schuster Speakers Bureau can bring authors to your
live event. For more information or to book an event, contact the
Simon & Schuster Speakers Bureau at 1-866-248-3049 or visit our
website at www.simonspeakers.com.

Acknowledgments

Special thanks to those who made this book possible. My agent, Brenda Hampton: you are the best. Lissa Woodson (Naleighna Kai): I don't know what I would have done without you. Charmaine Parker: thank you so much for working with me through the tight schedule.

Thank you Mom, Rachael, Chris, Lori, and Jeremy for supporting me from the very beginning. Thank you for your advice and honest opinions: Sheila, Asia, Terrell, and Sheneta. Thank you for inspiring me since childhood to write: Grandma Marocka, Uncle Andre, and Auntie Sholanda. Grandpa Morris: you always encouraged me to follow my passion.

Nikki Johnson pressed the Corvette's pedal to the metal, hoping to outrun the police who might be on her tail. She barely managed to keep her slippery palms on the steering wheel as she whipped up the shoulder of Interstate 10. The sports car topped one hundred miles per hour. Traffic wasn't heavy, but this was no racetrack, either. She needed to put as much space between her and Beverly Hills as possible and then come up with a plan.

"Oh my God!" she wailed as a blue car swerved into her path. Death flashed before her eyes; her heart slammed against her chest. Nikki jerked the wheel to avoid a front-to-back-end collision. Shifting into the next lane, she ignored the honks and protests of angry drivers as tires screeched and the smell of burnt rubber filled the smoggy air.

What am I going to do?

Everything passed by in a blur—as if frozen in time and she was the only one allowed to move. She squirmed in the driver's seat, the back of her sweaty thighs sticking to the leather. The reality of her fate continued to sink in, deeper and deeper. To say everything had caught up with her would be putting it mildly; karma had captured and executed her without giving ample warning.

I can't believe this is happening!

She pressed a palm against her forehead and wiped away the perspiration before it fell into her eyes. Ideas swarmed through her mind like bees around a hive, but only one made sense. *Run!*

But how was she going to get to Rayshad?

Forget him. You need to be worried about yourself.

How could she let that thought cross her mind? She couldn't abandon her son or let them take him away.

Worry pierced her stomach like a double-edged sword. California was a big place, but she would be a fool to think she could hide in the same state where she lived. Mexico seemed like a good idea. South of the border was only a few hours away.

Then it came to her out of nowhere. Her mother.

While concentrating on the road, she swept her long hair out of her face, then dove into her Louis Vuitton bag. Dialing her mother while steering a car treading over one hundred terrified her with each press of a button, but she couldn't slow down now.

"Hello?"

Nikki blinked back tears. "Ma? Ma, it's me!"

"Nikki, are you okay?"

Sobs tore out of Nikki's throat before she could rein them in. "Ma, Duncan is dead!"

"Wait a minute…"

"And they're coming for me, right now, Ma. I know it!"

"Hold on, slow down. *Who's* coming for you?"

"The police, Ma. I know I'm going down for this one. That's why I need you."

"*Me?*" Gina shrieked. "Why would you need me?"

Nikki wiped her eyes, clearing her vision. "I need you to tell them that I was somewhere else when everything happened."

When her mother didn't respond, Nikki bit her lip to keep from spilling out the truth and unburdening her soul. Instead, she got straight to the point. "I need you to be my alibi."

Chapter One

A Few Days Prior
November 9, 2007

D uncan Johnson unlatched the kitchen window and shoved it open. The cool breeze brought physical comfort, but did nothing to ease his mind. Seconds earlier, he had opened a small white envelope and discovered his fate.

YOU WILL DIE AND YOU KNOW WHY.

The message appeared to have been assembled with clippings from magazines and newspapers. Each letter had a different font, color, style, and background, neatly glued to the page.

His nose twitched at the spicy scent that radiated from the note. It was a perfume that was familiar, but hard to recollect. The page slipped from his sweaty fingers and fell onto the pile of mail beneath him on the marble counter.

Who was this mystery lady and why would she want him dead?

Closing his eyes, he recalled a collection of perfume on his wife's vanity. Nikki changed scents as often as she changed attire, which was several times a day.

She was no killer, though, and his wife was the last person he wanted to suspect. But after what had happened during the previous month, he began to wonder if this could be her way of paying him back for the pain he had caused.

☙ ☙ ☙

"Is Duncan here?"

Duncan heard the woman's voice echoing from the living room in his office two rooms over. He stood up from the desk, abandoning his computer to see who was at the front door.

"And who are you?" Nikki asked the lady.

"Are you Nikki?"

Marie! How did she find out where he lived?

Duncan rushed down the hallway with hopes that he would be able to explain everything to Nikki, but it was too late. Marie was already filling Nikki's ears with what he should have told her about three years earlier.

His seventeen-year-old stepson, Rayshad, lay across the couch with his legs crossed, ignoring the magazine in his lap, listening to their conversation.

"I know Duncan probably didn't tell you about me," she went on, "but my name is Marie, his baby's mother."

Nikki looked back and forth between the lady and small child. "Excuse me?"

Duncan stood quietly behind Nikki in the doorway frame of the hallway.

"That can't be possible," Nikki said. "Duncan doesn't have any children."

"Maybe not to *your* knowledge."

"How old is she?"

Marie adjusted the toddler on her hip and smiled down into the baby's face. "Demetria just turned three."

"What are you doing here?" Duncan slowly stepped out of the shadows.

Marie looked at Duncan with a twisted lip. "What am I doing here? I shouldn't have to play detective to get you to see your daughter." She stepped forward and shoved the little girl into Duncan's arms. "Her name is Demetria, in case you forgot."

Duncan looked at Nikki and tried to push the child back at Marie. "I—"

Nikki avoided eye contact with him. As the pain in her eyes grew, he felt compelled to make up some kind of excuse for the situation. Something that made sense.

Marie turned her back to them with a set of car keys jingling in her hand. "I expect that you'll be taking her shopping, since you haven't tried to do anything for her before."

Duncan bit his lip to keep from saying something he would regret. He wanted to follow Marie outside, yank her shoulders, and tell her to stay away from his home and his family, but it was his wife he needed to console.

Nikki grabbed the golden door handle. "Nice meeting you, Marie. Duncan will be calling you later on."

Marie parted her thin lips, but Nikki slammed the door in her face.

"Ma!" Demetria screamed.

Nikki stormed away as the baby wailed in his ear.

Duncan looked at his stepson helplessly. "Take her for me," he begged.

Rayshad rose from the couch and took the crying child from Duncan's grasp.

"Nikki…" He sprinted upstairs to catch up with her, but she pressed forward toward their bedroom.

"Don't even!" she warned.

Duncan tripped over a step and fell; pain shot through his knee. "Let me explain." He stood back up and heard the bedroom door slam shut. By the time he made it to the room, Nikki had already locked the door. He knocked. "Please let me in and at least hear me out."

"That baby is only three years old, Duncan," she cried from the other side of the door.

"Baby, I'm sorry. She's someone of my past, and I didn't know how to tell you."

Silence.

"Baby. Come on. I'll do anything to make this up to you."

When Nikki didn't say anything else, he threw his head back. He dreaded this day and cursed himself for being so careless. How did Marie find out where he stayed in the first place? Their community was gated. Who let her in and why?

"And you *will* be sleeping somewhere else, tonight!" Nikki added. "One of the guest rooms, on the couch— go sleep with Marie! But you won't be sleeping in bed with me."

❧ ❧ ❧

The more Duncan thought about the death threat, the more he realized that Marie had to be the one behind this nonsense. But was it something he really needed to be concerned about?

Duncan tucked the strange note in his back pocket, trashed what mail he didn't care for, and paced out of the chef's kitchen. Usually this time of day, when he arrived home from work, the aroma of another delicious meal greeted him followed by a kiss from Nikki. She usually took pride in being a housewife, but Marie's appearance had sent her into early retirement.

Walking slowly through the living room, he looked up at the high ceilings, plastered walls, and ornate carvings—all inspired by eighteenth-century France. A wonderful wife he had in Nikki as a gourmet chef, interior decorator, housekeeper, mother, and lover, but with each day that passed, he was losing the love of his life more and more.

Mixed emotions swirled through the pit of his stomach as he plopped down on a golden seat. Could Nikki be scorned enough to plot murder? She was neglecting her duties around the house, disappearing at odd times, and not returning his phone calls—all of which he accepted, taking into consideration how hurt she was. He was willing to stay in the doghouse as long as she didn't take things too far. But after what he'd discovered while analyzing the phone bill last night, her recent change in behavior all made sense. Nikki was fooling around with her ex-husband, Chance Brown.

Had to be. She hadn't spoken to him since the divorce seven years ago—not that Duncan knew of—but on October 8, 2007, shortly after the Marie situation, *she* started calling *him*, again.

Duncan dialed Nikki for the fourth time, rapidly tapping his foot on the plush rug as the cell phone rang. He had a feeling she was purposefully ignoring his calls. Was she with Chance? She definitely wasn't at her mother's house, because he'd already checked. That had been her excuse lately since they'd found out Gina had cancer.

The purr of an engine approaching from a distance snapped Duncan out of his thought pattern and he hung up the phone before leaving a voice message. Staring at the headlights coming closer through the fog, he swallowed with anticipation. But when the neighbor's black Bentley came into clear view, he slumped back on the couch.

He gazed into the cloudy sky, coming up with his own scenarios about where his wife could be at that moment. In Chance's arms. In his bed. He quickly shook away his thoughts and climbed to his feet. He refused to think Nikki was behind the death threat and didn't want to believe she was cheating on him with her ex-husband, either. After all, Chance was the father of her only son, so maybe their discussions were about Rayshad. Especially since the young man had been stressing Nikki over the past year. But why hadn't she told Duncan anything about their reunion?

A flash of lightning spread across the darkening sky and thunder erupted, echoing throughout the house. The news predicted bad weather, so he hoped Nikki was on her way home soon. But since he couldn't get in touch with her for the answers he wanted now, Duncan planned to ask Rayshad as soon as he got home from school.

Chapter Two

Chance reclined in the brown leather seat with his back turned to his desk and his eyes focused on a vibrant rainbow stretching across the cloud-filled sky. A black spider clung to an elaborate web that was slowly being decimated by the raindrops dripping at a steady pace.

His office was located on the fifteenth floor of one of the tallest buildings in the heart of downtown Los Angeles. There was nothing glamorous about the view—a bunch of old dirty buildings, busy streets, and countless numbers of homeless people wandering about. But it reminded him of the freedom he would have as soon as he completed his latest case. Being cooped up in the office all day and night, leaving only to eat and sleep, did not have its finer points. Neither was being a reputable attorney with too many clients to handle. Sometimes Chance wished he could go back to a time when one case was barely enough. That was before he had hit it big with the Clarkson trial fifteen years ago.

After meeting up with his co-counsel, he planned to

stop by a crime scene and check out a few things. Then he needed to speak with the defendant, a woman who allegedly murdered her husband and his mistress. And since his new intern didn't look like she was going to show up any time soon, he would have his secretary adjust his schedule for a shorter lunch break.

The squeaky-clean windows were shiny enough for him to see a reflection of the entire office behind him. Portraits of African-American political figures in thick black frames hung over the entryway. Dr. Martin Luther King Jr., Malcolm X, Thurgood Marshall, and the late Johnnie Cochran all reminded him of their persever-ance, which became a reflection of his own. He wondered if a year from now Barack Obama would actually be the first black President.

The intercom startled Chance out of a daze.

"Mr. Brown, you have a phone call on line three," Sylvia said softly through the intercom.

"One moment."

He swiveled his chair around to answer the phone and grimaced at the mess scattered across his desk. There was no way he would finish today. And another phone call was the last thing he needed. It was probably Olivia worrying him about their wedding plans, again. He glimpsed at a picture of her beautiful brown face, honey blonde hair, and chestnut eyes. It was halfway hidden behind a stack of files he had been sorting through earlier. Maybe he needed to cancel the lunch date with his fiancée altogether.

The intercom chimed in again.

"Mr. Brown?"

Chance leaned forward with his finger poised to click the blinking line. "Thanks, Sylvia."

"My pleasure, Mr. Brown," she replied, her tone both smooth and sultry.

Chance became instantly aroused—and not by his own will. The new secretary had been flirting with him all week. She was a cute Latina who wore tight outfits, but he tried his best to ignore her. He was engaged to one of the most powerful women in Los Angeles, the district attorney—not to mention, mayor's daughter. He couldn't afford one distraction at his office and had seen it too many times: men falling prey to workplace affairs only to be served up with million-dollar lawsuits so the "victims" could have some currency to wipe their fake tears on.

"Brown speaking."

"Hello, Chance."

His stomach tumbled. He knew that voice.

Glancing at his desk planner, he quickly calculated that it had been seven years. He picked up the receiver. "Nikki?"

"Hi."

"Hey." He loosened his tie, wondering how the cool air suddenly had become warm.

The last time they had talked, Nikki's voice dripped with such contempt that Chance kept his distance and words short. Seven years after the divorce, it was as if their eleven-year marriage never existed. She now had a new man, a new life, and Chance did not weigh in—not even for Rayshad.

"What's going on, Nikki?"

"Nothing much. How are you?"

"Fine. Fine."

He honed in, listening to see if any background noise could clue him in to the reason for the call. Silence on the other end sparked his curiosity. "Is everything all right?"

"I just…"

There was a long pause and Chance swallowed hard, trying to make the lump in his throat disappear. Had she heard about his engagement to Olivia?

"I was calling to see how you've been doing these past few years," she continued.

He switched the phone to his other ear and swiveled the chair so he had an outside view again. "I'm surprised that you're even concerned."

"Why do you say that?"

Chance chuckled, but didn't answer her question. "No. I'm really glad you called." Glancing over his shoulder at the computer, he realized that he was already behind schedule, but didn't care.

"Are you really?" Nikki asked dryly.

"Yeah," he said calmly, but inside, the adrenaline rush he felt was as powerful—if not more—than the way he'd felt when first meeting her in college. Simply seeing her could make his heart stop then. He wondered what she looked like now.

The spider outside of his window was barely hanging onto the last strands of the web, prompting him to pull the vertical blinds shut against its inevitable demise. "So how's life been for you? How's Rayshad?"

"Rayshad's doing good. He's an honor student," she gushed. "Got a new car for his sixteenth birthday. Had a little girlfriend for a while, but they broke up not too long ago."

"Girlfriend, huh?" His son was old enough for a car and a girlfriend. He had missed so much.

"Yeah. She was nice, and really pretty, too. Smart—but I guess things didn't work out for them."

Chance stole a glance at Olivia's photo. "And what about you? How's *your* love life been?"

"I've been hanging in there. Been married for almost seven years now."

"*Seven?* When…" Chance tried to keep his cool. He felt slightly betrayed that she had remarried so quickly after their divorce. He was in no position to point fingers, because it didn't take long for him to move on. But not to anything serious. Chance had enjoyed being single for those few years before meeting Olivia.

"I hope he's treating you right," he said with sincerity.

There was nothing but silence on the other end.

"Is he?"

Nikki still didn't reply for several moments, and when she did, it was only: "I can tell you this…"

"What?" He swallowed hard, hoping that this man— her *husband*—had better not have harmed her or his son.

"I'm not happy, Chance."

A rush went through Chance's body and the love he felt for Nikki made him want to rescue her. But, common sense told him that Nikki had somehow heard about his engagement, which put him on alert. What other reason could there be for a call this late in the game? If she was unhappy this week, then she had been unhappy months before. Why not call then?

He opened his mouth to speak, but before he could get a word out, Nikki said, "I heard you're getting married."

"Oh really?" He rubbed his forehead, wondering how she'd found out—not that it mattered. "Is that why you called?"

"No. Wanted to talk to you, that's all. Haven't heard from you since the divorce."

"Talk?" he said, trying to keep the bitterness from his voice. "What about?"

"To see if you were okay. Wanted to take you out to lunch actually...*if* that's okay with you."

Chance was taken aback. He thought all of this time Nikki would resent him for not making an effort to see or support their son. Why was she so interested in him again?

"When? Today?"

"Yeah. Right now. Our old spot. Mia Bella."

Chance looked at his watch and revisited his schedule. Olivia would kill him if he canceled their lunch date to go cake tasting. But something in him couldn't resist. "I'll see you there."

He disconnected the call and took a deep breath. His heart was still beating fast as though he had run a full marathon during their short conversation. The sensation in his pants told him that he missed Nikki in more than one way. Then his mind went into overdrive: Would she look differently? Had she gained weight? Did she have another child? Was she in love with that man?

He grabbed his keys and ignored Sylvia as he breezed toward the lobby.

"Mr. Brown? Where are you going? Don't forget you have a meeting with Fred in an hour."

To hell with his appointments! He wasn't focused enough to do anything else. Hearing Nikki's voice brought back memories. Of course he hadn't forgotten about her. The degrees and licenses matted and framed on the walls of his office represented not only his hard work, but the fact that Nikki had been his backbone and main supporter on his journey from college basketball star to successful attorney. She might have had flaws in other areas, but she'd held down the homefront like his mother had growing up. And her cooking! He couldn't pay a woman to take pleasure in cooking for her man like Nikki did. A lot more than he could say about Olivia. His fiancée had taken the liberty of hiring a chef and a maid— on his dime!

Where did everything start going wrong with their relationship? he thought as he hopped into his BMW. Especially since he'd met her during one of the best times of his life.

🐌 🐌 🐌

Three sips past drunk, Chance staggered into the sophomore dormitory on the UCLA campus and dragged himself upstairs to his room. Music from the '87 New Year's frat party still rang in his ears as he slid a key into the door. Or was that his roommate listening to the radio?

He tried to push the door open, but a damp towel blocking the way made it difficult. A Prince ballad played softly from the boombox in the corner. Smoke from burning incense and the pungent scent of marijuana hovered in the air.

Flipping the switch, he found that one of his posters had fallen from the wall. A big picture of Public Enemy, which normally hung next to those of Slick Rick, N.W.A, and MC Lyte, was face down on the ground—right next to a purple bra with cups that would barely hold a drink of water.

His roommate hadn't even heard him come in. He was too busy sucking the face of a topless girl in his bed.

"My fault, man," Chance said as he inched backward, almost tripping over a pile of dirty clothes.

The lovers pulled away from one another. She wiped her lips with the back of her red manicured hand, then slipped toward the edge of the bed. Boldly looking into Chance's eyes, she snatched the blouse from the floor.

He couldn't tear his gaze from her small perky breasts

and soon got the vibe that she didn't care about his gawking. She took her time clipping her bra on.

"Don't apologize," she said casually, almost smiling.

Chance nodded, then glanced at Johnny cheesing harder than in his third-grade school photo. If his roommate managed to get someone as gorgeous as this girl in bed, then why hadn't he asked her to bring a friend?

She smoothed lipstick across her full lips and tossed the tube back into her handbag. Chance followed her movements as she pranced across the room to retrieve the Prince cassette in the boombox. Even though she was fully dressed, he still held the topless vision of her in his mind.

"You said I can have this, right?" she asked Johnny, placing the cassette in her purse.

"Yeah. It's all yours," he replied, smoothing a hand over his high-top fade.

Chance didn't have a moment to protest that it was actually his tape, but he would make sure his roommate bought another.

"All right, well, I'm gone." Nikki stepped forward. "It was nice meeting you...Chance, right?"

He looked down at his shoulder as she brushed against him. "Yeah. And you are?"

"Nikki." She smiled and waved her fingers at him flirtatiously. "Bye."

Chance watched her short skirt sway side to side as she walked out of the door.

"Is she dope, man, or what?" When Chance didn't respond, Johnny threw a pillow at his head to wake him out of his daze.

"No doubt, man," Chance replied, shaking it off. All the while his gears were clicking, trying to figure out how to get at Nikki.

After several secret dates to the movies, dinner, and walks in the park, Chance won her over. Johnny was furious when he found out, but Chance wasn't trying to hear it. Johnny had helped himself to Chance's food, clothes, and shoes even, and never made much fuss about it. But giving away his *Purple Rain* soundtrack was going above the line. Prince's music was solid. Fair exchange was no robbery.

Two years into their relationship, Nikki invited him over her apartment for dinner to give him the most disturbing news of his life at that time.

She seemed a little more quiet than usual, but he thought she was letting him watch the game without much interruption.

"Baby, I have something to tell you."

Chance stuffed a fried chicken wing in his mouth. "What's up?" he mumbled, but his eyes were still glued to the NBA Playoffs. "What?!" he screamed at the television. "Aw, nah, man."

She stroked a hand across his broad chest. "Are you listening to me, Chance?"

"Yeah, yeah, yeah," he replied quickly. "Did you see that, though?"

"Chance, I'm pregnant."

He froze. The basketball game, sounds and all, faded to the background. "What?"

"I'm pregnant, baby," Nikki cried out.

Chance shook his head and slapped a hand across his forehead. Images of a promising basketball career flushed down a giant-sized toilet. After leading his high school team to the '84 state championship, and now making great advances on the college level, how could he have let this happen? And with graduation in a month? A baby? What was he going to do?

Nikki's sobbing cut in the background of his thoughts. The last thing he would do was neglect his responsibilities. His father had married his mother a few years before starting their family. What would his parents think if he didn't live by the values they had instilled in him at a young age? He vowed to be like his parents, but expected the "family" thing to happen long after college and playing ball overseas.

Chance pulled Nikki close, trying to provide some sense of comfort, even though he needed some of his own. He remembered the first time he had slept with her. Initially, he planned to rendezvous once, maybe twice, then move on to the next girl. But Nikki was different from the average one-night stand. The sex was out of this world, her body was banging, and the way she carried herself complemented his basketball star status. More than anything, she always put him first.

His roommate had a child on the way by a girl he

claimed was lying, but that was the last thing that crossed Chance's mind with Nikki. He had no choice but to take responsibility for what had happened, because he hated condoms and had assumed she was still on the pill. As much as they tumbled in the sheets, this would have happened long before now if she hadn't been on something.

But he knew it was all up to him. His father would raise hell if he didn't handle the situation like a man.

Lifting Nikki's chin, he looked her in the eyes, swallowed his doubts, and let his heart lead him in the right decision. "We need to get married, then."

"Are you sure?" she asked, relief flowing into her eyes as he wiped her tears away.

Chance pressed his lips together and pushed against the heaviness weighing on his chest. "Yeah. I think so."

Calling the talent scout to decline his offer was the hardest thing Chance ever had to do. But, there was no way he would work overseas, thousands of miles away from his wife and child.

ॐ ॐ ॐ

An hour after the call to his downtown office, Nikki walked through the door of Mia Bella—fashionably late as usual. Chance almost didn't recognize her since her naturally curly hair had been straightened and was now swinging down her back. As he examined her sexy, slim physique, he was quickly reminded that Nikki cared too much about maintaining a healthy body to let herself go.

And her breasts, were they…bigger?

He stood up and met her at the door. "You look beautiful." His gaze swept over her body and he blinked twice. She practically looked like a different person.

Tossing her hair over her shoulder, she turned around and allowed Chance to remove her jacket. "Thank you. You don't look too bad yourself."

"*Too* bad?" he teased, smoothing his forty-year-old hand across the back of his head. "The gray hairs are showing that much?"

Nikki narrowed her eyes and only then did she notice sparkly, silver bits along his thinning hairline. "They say that's a sign of wisdom," she replied evenly.

Chance handed her jacket to the hostess and guided Nikki to the table he had kept warm for almost thirty minutes before she'd arrived. "That's what I hear. Call me a realist, call me a pessimist; I see them as a sign of age."

Nikki gave him an intense look. "I was trying to give you a little credit," she replied as he poured a glass of wine for her from a half-empty bottle he'd downed during the wait. "Or should I say—I was hoping you'd wised up a bit. You didn't make the best decisions toward the end of our marriage."

Chance's eyebrows shot up; an embarrassed smile on his face. "I deserved that. You're right. But now that you're here, I was hoping that I could make all of that up to you."

Nikki picked up her wineglass. "We both made mistakes. I will admit that," she replied, dismissing that part of their lives with a flourish of her hand. "But now's not the time to worry about the past." She raised her glass. "Here's to new fate."

His eyes stayed focused on her eyes as he touched his glass to hers. "To new fate."

Mesmerized by her beauty, Chance couldn't recall how the food had tasted that day or even what they had talked about. So many years had passed and he hadn't laid eyes on her. This sudden reappearance made him realize how much he'd really missed her. Out of all the women he'd been with, Nikki topped them all.

Chance scanned her face and shook his head. She always put so much detail into her makeup, and didn't need any of it to enhance her natural beauty. His gaze continued downward over every inch of her perfectly sculpted frame. With her long legs exposed, he wondered what kind of panties she had on. Or if she had on any at all.

His mind suddenly drifted to thoughts of Olivia and how he had cancelled with her to be with Nikki. Even though Olivia had status, what he felt for her did not compare to the love he felt for Nikki. Inwardly, he had hopes of rekindling some type of relationship with Nikki, but still wondered why she had insisted on seeing him.

Chance grabbed her hand. Soft fingers. Long nails—

almost as long as Olivia's. That was something different, too. She never wore them long because it would interfere with her passion for cooking. Were they real? He had figured by now that her breasts had to be implants.

Glancing at her hand, he could make out the light shadings on her skin indicating she had removed her jewelry. He wondered what kind of ring her husband had given her.

"I really do miss you," Nikki said toward the end of the date. "And I've been needing to get away for a while, now. Why don't we plan a weekend getaway? Take a trip somewhere close like Vegas. My treat."

His brow furrowed at the thought. Her treat? That meant her husband would actually be footing the bill. He took a small bit of pleasure in that fact. This Duncan fellow had taken what rightfully belonged to Chance, so to have his money finance their reconnection was an ironic twist of fate.

Chapter Three

Chance was at the front desk of Bally's Las Vegas Resort & Casino when Nikki gracefully stepped into the lobby at a half past six in the evening. She flung her hair over her shoulders, removed her shades and locked a steady gaze on him, sashaying as though she owned the world. He was used to her wearing skirts and dresses, but she looked stunning in an off-shoulder blouse and some of the tightest, thinnest pants he had seen on her. He was also used to her wearing bright colors. Instead she wore all black, but the red soles of her Christian Louboutin pumps shined as if she had trotted through a trail of blood.

"Hey," she beamed. A busboy followed behind her, rolling four large Louis Vuitton luggage bags. "Sorry, I'm a little late." Reaching in her purse, she pulled something out and handed it to Chance. "Here."

Without looking down, he knew it was the money she had mentioned. Chance covered her hand and curled her palm around the cash.

"It's for the room," she insisted. "I told you the trip was on me."

"Since you had me reserve the room, I'm charging it to my card." Contrary to what he felt about her husband, he couldn't rightly take the man's money the way the man had taken his wife.

She tucked the wad of bills into her pocketbook and followed him toward the elevators.

Upon settling into the room, Nikki dumped all of her makeup and perfume bottles on the vanity and organized them neatly in front of the mirror. A sweet aroma filled the room as she unpacked her belongings—a smell Chance used to breathe in from her neck when they made love. He hadn't realize how much he missed that scent.

"Dinner's in an hour," she said, gliding into the bathroom with a garment bag.

He knew too well how long it took for Nikki to dress. All he needed was fifteen minutes, even though his original plan was to go to dinner wearing the same Ralph Lauren polo shirt and jeans he wore while traveling. But since she was going out of her way to get dolled up, he matched her style with an Armani shirt and dress pants. He almost forgot that he didn't bring his bottle of cologne and a few other items that Olivia might have noticed missing, but the scent still lingered on him.

The bathroom door didn't open until forty-five minutes later. Nikki stepped out in a purple dress that put her new breasts on display and sauntered across the room to return items to her luggage. "Wow. You look great." Her entire back was exposed, accentuating her round behind.

She zipped her bag closed. "Thank you."

He grabbed the hotel key, hoping they could still make their dinner reservation, but Nikki sat before the vanity and grabbed a long makeup brush. Like an artist, she rubbed it against a palette, leaned into the mirror, and started stroking above her lashes. Her face was her canvas.

"I still don't understand why you wear all of that makeup," he said, walking up behind her. He rubbed her shoulders. "You are gorgeous the way you are."

"Thank you, baby." She smiled at him through the mirror. "This won't take me but a minute. I know we're late."

But that minute turned into another hour.

❦❧ ❧ ❧

Nikki placed a dark red strawberry dipped in milk chocolate right on the tip of Chance's full lips. His eyes rolled into the back of his head as it melted in his mouth. He moaned, "Mmmnn!"

"Good, huh?" Nikki smiled warmly. The night's breeze combed through her shiny, dark hair.

"Not as good as you."

She giggled. "Ooh. You're bad."

With his eyes still closed, the expression on Chance's face conveyed pure bliss as he took in the sweet fragrance of Nikki's perfume. The meal paled in comparison to her cooking, but even if she had cooked for him, he would have still been distracted by her presence. She had just turned thirty-eight and it was as though a single year hadn't touched Nikki since meeting her in college.

The taste of a savory filet mignon lingered even though they were on dessert; dining in seclusion on the rooftop of a casino. One of the waiters approached the table, refilling their glasses with Dom Pérignon. Nikki had already toasted to the rekindling of their relationship as if he had plans of calling the wedding off to reunite with her. He took a large gulp of champagne and tried not to think about Olivia who had just sent him a text message stating that she was on her way to get her bridesmaids fitted.

Tunes from Sade's *Love Deluxe* album played quietly in the background. Two lattice partitions adorned with small white lights added to the décor of dark green foliage, exotic plants, and glowing candles strategically placed to create a romantic mood.

Nikki really outdid herself.

"Cherish the Day" drifted from hidden speakers, taking him back to '92. Times were good for them back then. He was broke and had struggled to make ends meet as a full-time law student, but somehow had managed. He bobbed his head to the hypnotizing bass. They used to play the hell out of that cassette!

As Chance leaned back in the seat watching her smile back at him, doubt crept in. What would the future hold now that Nikki was back in his life? Olivia had already hired an expensive wedding planner and sent the invitations to their friends and family. They were well into a full-scale event. And he had to wonder with Nikki: was this a new beginning or a continuation of their troubled past? They'd had more bad times than good, but seven years apart might have given her time to appreciate what they once had. But on the flipside, it might put a spotlight on the many things that went wrong; things they had never discussed.

Suddenly, fireworks blasted through the starless sky.

Leaning back in his chair, he peered through the candle's flame at Nikki's beautiful features, which seemed to take on an angelic glow. Vibrant lights from the surrounding casinos trailing up the strip provided the perfect backdrop.

"So many memories," she whispered as she flashed her lighter and took a long pull of a Virginia Slim.

"Remember when we got married here?" he asked. "We had no money. Not for a real wedding."

She released a trail of smoke that danced in the air and slowly disappeared. "We just had each other and that old Pontiac of yours."

Chance laughed. "It made it all the way here and back to L.A. before it died a year later."

"But after you won the Clarkson trial, you finally moved us from Altadena to Bel Air, got your BMW, and then the Tahoe for my twenty-seventh birthday."

Chance nodded, but his cheerful expression slowly faded. "You're rolling big time now. A flashy Corvette?"

She shrugged. "Hey, I live life in the fast lane."

"Then stop giving me the red light." He winked as she giggled.

Nikki was always such a tease.

Her cell phone began ringing and she looked up at Chance. Embarrassment flushed her light brown skin to bright red. This was the fourth time the phone had gone off in the past ten minutes.

Chance cleared his throat loudly.

She laughed nervously and held her phone up. "Rayshad."

He sat back in his chair and shook his head, knowing that was her husband calling. Only a man who felt entitled to know a woman's every move would call her repeatedly back-to-back. Jealousy boiled within him before another thought occurred: was this her first affair? Was this how she had handled him when their relationship was coming to a screeching halt? Hushed conversations? Lapses in memory? Time she couldn't account for?

He polished off the rest of the champagne, trying not to let his insecurities get the best of him. After all, Nikki no longer belonged to him, so there really wasn't anything he could say.

"How *is* Rayshad?" He started back on the chocolate-covered strawberries before him.

"He's doing good." Nikki crushed the last of her cigarette in the ashtray.

"Has he been behaving? Does he still have that smart mouth?"

"No," she answered defensively.

"Yeah right. I bet he's still calling you by your first name."

Nikki smirked. "No. But he still calls *you* by *yours*."

Chance wiped his mouth with a napkin. "You need to teach that boy the meaning of respect before he starts running all over you."

"That *boy* you are referring to is now a *man*. Maybe you'd know that if you actually spent time with him. He's seventeen, just in case you've forgotten. And, he knows his place!"

"Talking back is going over the line. Not doing what you say is unacceptable. You treat him like he's your friend, not your child."

"Don't sit here and critique my parenting skills." She pointed a finger at him. "It's been seven years since we divorced, and you haven't even made an attempt to get in touch with him."

"Yeah." Chance smoothed his mustache with his thumb and index finger, wondering how this argument had even started. "I've thought about him over the years. I know I haven't reached out, but I knew he was in good hands."

"If you cared, you would have at least called."

"I care about Rayshad. I care about both of you. But Nikki, you know why things are the way they are. Trina told me—"

Nikki tossed her napkin on the table. "You've got your nerve bringing her up."

"See, Nikki. This is what I'm talking about right here. You'll hang that over my head for the rest of my life, but won't cop to your faults."

"We all do things when we're young, but you crossed the line with that one."

"And how many lines did you cross?"

Nikki's fingers touched her temples. "I'm not here to argue with you, Chance."

"What *are* you here for, Nikki?"

Her almond eyes looked heavenward and filled with tears. "Because I love you and I miss you and Rayshad misses you."

He wiped his face, growing more uncomfortable with each second that passed. Is this why she wanted a weekend getaway? So she could push him in a corner and confront him? He downed the rest of his champagne. "If you wanted to start out with a clean slate, you wouldn't be harping on things in the past."

She patted her tears with a napkin and crossed her arms. "You brought up Trina."

"And I'm glad I brought her up, because I'm beginning to question why I'm even here."

As he scooted his seat back to stand, Nikki's eyes grew. "Chance, calm—"

"I love Rayshad; don't get me wrong. But every time I hear his name, I think about your lies."

Nikki looked another direction.

"And you don't have anything to say?"

"Say like what?" She batted her eyes.

"Don't worry about it." Chance stood from his seat and threw a few bills on the table. "Some things just don't change."

"What are you doing?" she asked as he walked away from the table.

He didn't realize that she had followed behind him until she pulled his hand.

"Stop," she begged.

"No, Nikki. I wasn't the perfect husband. But when I did something wrong, I apologized about it. You can't even do that."

"But I *am* sorry, Chance. Come sit down. Please. The waiters are looking at us."

Chance still wouldn't move.

"You are right. I was wrong," she said impatiently, looking around. "But I never got an apology from you about Trina, either."

"No, because you left out of nowhere. Next thing I know, your attorney is serving me divorce papers."

Nikki wrapped her arms around him. "Let's sit back down and talk this over like rational adults." She looked up into his eyes. "Don't be mad. We're here to enjoy ourselves."

Chance exhaled. "Only if you can be real with me," he bargained.

Nikki grabbed his hand and tried to guide him back to the table, but he pulled his hand from her grasp. "Is what Trina told me true?"

She turned around to face him but quickly looked away.

"Am I Rayshad's father or not?"

Chapter Four

"So how do you like it?" Nikki asked, pouring lemonade from a plastic pitcher into two glasses. Long, thick braids trailed down her flat chest.

Trina Campbell's wide nose sniffed as she grabbed her cup and poured a lot of sugar in it. "It's…it's nice," she replied, looking around. Her eyes stopped at a spot with peeling wallpaper.

Nikki pursed her lips. She noticed how her best friend refrained from complimenting their small Altadena home. They weren't living in a luxurious neighborhood like Trina was accustomed to, but Nikki took pride in their small home, decorating each room with cheap furniture and decor that at best appeared to be expensive.

"Yeah, we got it for a deal," Nikki carried on, closing her purple robe. She tied her braids back in a ponytail. "Chance says we should have it paid off in fifteen years."

Trina frowned. "You guys plan on staying here *that* long?"

"If we need to," she glowered, placing her hands on her hips. "You say that like something's wrong with this place."

Trina leaned on her arms over the counter. "It's not that." She looked around distastefully. "I'm just saying, before Chance came into your life, you had all these high standards for men. They have to have this, and they have to be able to do that. The way you used to talk, I knew you were going to marry a millionaire." Her eyes fell on Nikki's golden band that had no diamonds on it.

Nikki rolled her eyes and moved her hand out of Trina's view. Since they met as college roommates, Trina always bragged about her designer clothes, bags, jewels, and boyfriends who had money until Nikki had once felt compelled to lie just to feel accepted. But not anymore.

"Girl, who cares about money when you have a man who loves you like Chance loves me?"

"Money don't pay the bills, honey."

"Before it's all said and done, Chance *will* be a millionaire," Nikki replied confidently. "I didn't tell you that he was accepted into law school?"

Trina hid her reaction behind a sip of lemonade. "That's nice."

"Yeah. His plan is to become an attorney and have his own practice one day."

"And *your* plan? What are your dreams, Nikki?"

"*My* plan is to be the best wife I can be. Chance needs a strong woman in his corner."

"So that whole barefoot and pregnant thing—that's you? Girl, it's the eighties, and about to be the nineties! Women don't have to be housewives no more, running around cooking and cleaning and taking care of a house full of kids. You better ask somebody."

"Corporate America is not for everybody, Trina."

"Still." Trina rolled her eyes. "Taking care of a man?" Trina scoffed. "Having a house filled with his children? Not working? You mean to tell me you wasted thousands of dollars in student loans to go to school and not finish your degree? And say he does get all this money. What if he leaves you for another woman? What money will *you* have to fall back on?"

Nikki opened her mouth to reply, but Chance opened the side door and walked inside.

Dressed in a tank top and pants, his body was drenched in sweat, evidence of a hard day of cutting grass. He used the bottom of his shirt to wipe his wet face. "Hey, Trina."

"What's up?"

"Nothing much," he replied and turned to Nikki. "Pour me a glass of that lemonade. Will you, honey?"

Nikki was already closing the refrigerator with a full glass in her hand before he had finished his sentence. "Here you go, baby. You finished out there?"

Chance sucked the entire drink within a few seconds.

Trina watched him sourly.

He slammed the glass down, breathing hard, and wiped his forehead, again. "Thank you, baby."

Nikki gave him a kiss.

"I'm guessing she already told you the news," Chance said to Trina.

Trina looked at Nikki and back at Chance.

He placed his hand over Nikki's lower belly. "We're about to have a baby."

Trina's eyes widened. "Get outta here!"

Nikki smiled nervously. "Yep."

"Girl, why didn't you tell me?"

"I just...I just didn't." Nikki sighed and poured her husband another glass of lemonade. "I wanted to wait until the time was right."

Trina's eyebrows elevated. "Well, congratulations," she replied flatly. "I guess that means you won't be able to go to the Devontae concert with me." She pulled two tickets out of her purse. "I got tickets and knew you would wanna go."

Nikki's covered her mouth and squealed. She looked from the tickets to Chance and back to Trina. "Oh my God, Chance, can I go?"

Trina puffed.

"Of course," Chance replied. "Why not?"

Nikki kissed him on the cheek. "Thanks, baby. When is it?"

"This weekend." Trina clicked her nails on the counter.

Chance grabbed his glass. "Well, have fun." He started toward the living room. "I'm about to hop in the shower."

Trina rolled her eyes as he exited the room.

🐾 🐾 🐾

Slipping into a booth across from Nikki with a Martini glass in her hand, Trina looked around the crowded after-party for Devontae. The spot was packed wall-to-wall with people bumping into one another traveling to the bar and dance floor. Trina twisted her torso to the beat with her arms in the air, fingers snapping.

Nikki eyed Trina's pink drink with a lime floating on top. "Where's mine?" she asked, speaking loudly over the background music and noise.

Trina kept dancing as she sipped from the Martini glass, crinkling her face. "What? You're pregnant, girl. Why on earth would you want to drink?"

Nikki grabbed Trina's Cosmopolitan and took a large gulp. "Girl, please. I'm not *really* pregnant. I just told Chance that."

Trina fell back into her seat. "Why would you do that?"

Nikki waved her hand forward. "I'll tell you later."

"Later? No girl, we need to talk about this now. What's gotten into you with all these secrets you've been keeping from me?"

"I haven't been keeping anything from you."

"You kept *this* from me."

"Big deal, girl. It's not even that serious."

Trina crossed her arms. "You don't think so?"

"No."

"Well, tell me this: when did you tell him you were pregnant?"

"A couple of months ago. Why?"

"Are you serious?" Trina choked on her drink. "You mean to tell me that you told Chance this *before* you got married?"

"It's not that I haven't been *trying* to get pregnant since we got married. I *have*. It just won't happen."

"It's not a matter of you trying to get pregnant, Nikki. You told Chance this so he would marry you, didn't you?"

"Not really, I—"

Trina held up her hand to hush Nikki. "You do realize that even if you were to get pregnant *tonight*, the dates would nowhere near match up?"

Nikki leaned forward. "Don't tell Chance." She took another sip of her friend's drink.

"Oh, you know I won't. But, he'll find out sooner or later."

Nikki shrugged her shoulders, slinging her braids back. "Well, I'll deal with that situation when it arises. Until then, I'm not worried about it." She scooted out of the booth, adjusted her dress, and slipped through the crowd to the bar.

She returned a few minutes later with two drinks, handing one to Trina. "Now, let me get a cigarette," she said. "I haven't bought any since Chance and I've been married."

Trina's eyebrows rose. "I wouldn't want you smoking either if I thought you were pregnant." She handed Nikki the cigarette and lighter.

"Where's Devontae?" Nikki asked, looking around the

crowd. Holding her cigarette up elegantly, she inhaled the tip.

Trina hummed. "I dunno."

"We've been here forever. How much longer will it be?" Her original plan was to go to the concert and head back home, but Trina found out about the after-party, which rumored Devontae's appearance. "Girl, I'm ready to go." Nikki yawned. "It's *way* past my curfew, anyway."

Trina crushed her cigarette in an ashtray that had barely enough room for any more butts. "Damn, girl! Chance has you whipped like that?"

"You wish your man cared about you like mine does," Nikki snapped. "It's just a concert. I had fun. Now it's time to go."

Trina nudged her friend. "Come on, now. You know how famous folks are! Always late to their own parties. He's probably outside in a limo, right now."

"Whatever, girl. I'm ready to go home to my husband. I'm so damn tired of all these dudes eyeballing me. I swear!"

"You?" Trina rolled her eyes. "Girl, I'm pissed off that all these men are doing is staring. Not one person has approached me. And I know I look good."

Nikki blinked at Trina's curly hair, red dress, and gold accessories. "We might as well go. There's nothing really going on here, anyway."

"Wait, girl," Trina encouraged.

Nikki threw her hand up. "For what? I'm tired. It's been

a couple of hours, and Devontae *still* hasn't showed up!"

She crossed her arms when she realized her friend wasn't paying her any attention. Trina had become hypnotized by something behind Nikki.

She frowned and turned to see what had Trina so entranced. A man in all black and dark shades stood behind her, looking like security. Nikki looked him up and down. "Yes, can we help you?"

"Yeah," he replied. "Devontae would like to see you." He turned to Trina. "Both of you ladies."

"For real?" Trina giggled with excitement.

Nikki remained calm and nodded. "Devontae?" She scanned the entire club. "Where is he? I haven't seen him all night."

"Come with me," he instructed.

Nikki stood and downed the rest of her drink. "That's cool, I guess. We were just about to leave, anyway."

Trina grabbed her purse and hopped out of her seat. "I told you to be patient. See?"

"Oh my God!" Nikki exclaimed as they followed the man to the other side of the room. "I can't believe Devontae wants *us* to sit with him! Can you believe that, girl?"

Trina stood tall. "Doesn't surprise me, really."

The guard escorted them to a secluded area Nikki had never paid attention to. She had no idea that this club had a V.I.P. area. She could finally see Devontae from a distance. Loud colors decorated his outlandish outfit; a costume that only an entertainer would be caught dead in. Yellow skin and pink lips. He reminded her of Chance. His hair, however, was long, relaxed, and curled at the ends like a woman. Or a pimp.

As they approached Devontae's table, Trina's excitement faded. Two bombshells were already sitting on both sides of him. They glared at Nikki and Trina.

Devontae smiled. "Ladies…" He snapped his fingers twice. The two women sitting next to him stood up and walked away. His eyes locked on Nikki. "Have a seat."

Nikki looked at Trina and nodded. "That's what I'm talking about!"

"Have we met?" Devontae asked Nikki as she slid into the booth next to him. His eyes raced all over her body in a tight, lavender dress that exposed her shoulders, chest, and back.

"Only in my dreams." Nikki laughed.

"Ha-ha! Something told me I knew you from somewhere." He snatched his cognac glass resembling a fishbowl from the table and cradled it in his hand. He looked at Trina who was sitting on the other side of him and smirked. "You with her?"

Trina nodded excitedly. "Mmm-hmm."

"Oh, aight." Then he turned back to Nikki. "So, Miss—" He stopped short, waiting for Nikki to fill in the blank.

She smiled. "Well, actually, it's more like Miss-*es*…I'm married."

"Miss—Mrs.—I don't give a damn. Fine as you are… shit, I might take you away from ya man, ya dig?"

Nikki's eyebrows rose. She could hardly understand what he had slurred. The way his eyes fluttered, she wondered what else had he been doing besides drinking.

"I'm single!" Trina sang from the other side.

Devontae looked up, but didn't bother turning around. "But like I was sayin', girl...you got it goin' on! With a body like that, let me guess: you dance."

Nikki's eyebrows rose as she shook her head.

"If you play it cool, I can see about putting you in my next video. You would love to come on tour wit' ya man, wouldn't you?"

She shook her head. "I—"

"Seems like I've seen you in a club somewhere or on a music video already."

"Not me. I told you before, I don't dance. And I'm married."

"And?" Devontae spoke with his hands, which were decorated with gold jewelry. "A brother like me...I can wine you, dine you, show you the world. I told you...I don't give a damn about what's goin' on at home. What I need to know is what's goin' on between me and you. Now, how does that sound?"

She looked across Devontae to her best friend who had her lips poked out. Trina rolled her eyes enviously. Nikki shrugged her shoulders and tilted her head to the side as if to say, *'What do you expect me to do, say no?'*

Trina shook her head and looked the other way.

Nikki giggled at Devontae and sipped her drink. "I haven't been around the world before."

"Yeah," he said, adjusting himself in the booth.

Nikki noticed how he had purposefully repositioned himself to put emphasis on the large lump in his pants.

"I knew you would," he replied vainly. "Shit, I've been around the world and back, got big cars and houses, millions of fans young and old, and I don't sing about bein' good in bed for nothing!"

Nikki listened to Devontae talk about himself all night. Each drink numbed her thoughts to a point that Chance no longer crossed her mind.

"All right!" Devontae sat up and clapped twice. A waiter came by and he ordered another round of drinks for everyone in the area. "Keep 'em comin'!" he shouted. "My lady over here looks thirsty!" He wrapped his arm around Nikki and pulled her closer to him.

Nikki giggled at the animated entertainer and took her next shot of alcohol. Her mind soared to another level of highness and everything seemed to be a dream.

Devontae whispered something in her ear as Trina eyed her from the other side.

And that was the last memory she had of that night.

Chapter Five

P eeling her eyes open, Nikki looked around, dumbfounded by the unfamiliar surroundings. They were exquisite, nonetheless, and something like a fancy hotel suite. Sitting up, she scratched her hair, realizing the throbbing pain in her forehead. A bad taste foamed in her mouth followed by the simmering urge to throw up. Then again, maybe not, but her stomach still roiled.

The smell of alcohol, cologne, and morning breath reeked from the snoring body next to her. She gasped. "Oh my God," she cried out quietly. Looking down at her wedding band, she cursed. Her night with Devontae wasn't a dream.

Nikki held her breath as he rolled over in his sleep and continued to snore. She never thought she would be grossed out, lying in bed with a celebrity she once adored.

Climbing out of bed, she scurried across the room and bundled her clothes that were scattered about. Holding them to her chest, she ran to the restroom to relieve the returning urge to throw up. How did she drink herself into a hangover? Chance would have a fit if he knew she'd drunk alcohol the night before. She buried her face in the toilet. A hangover would be the least of his worries, if he knew where she was. She wiped her mouth with the back of her hand and turned on the shower.

While lathering her body with soap, she wondered about Trina and her whereabouts—hopefully somewhere close to her and far away from Chance. He was probably at home pissed off, ready to curse her out, but she could trust Trina not to rat her out. Not intentionally, at least.

She scrubbed her soapy body as hard as she could, but the shower didn't wash away her shame. Three months of marriage hadn't passed and she was already an adulteress. Tears poured over her already wet face as she cried silently. Never did she think she would break her vows with Chance. Cheaters can't possibly love their mates, she once thought, but she was in love with him even more than the day they got married. How could she be so foolish?

Wrapping herself in a towel, she stepped outside of the bathroom quietly. Devontae was still in bed snoring.

The bedroom door creaked as she poked her head into the living room, scanning over the leather couches and adjoining kitchen. This penthouse suite was fabulous and something she had only seen on television. But with betraying Chance weighing heavily on her heart, she was hardly impressed.

Another door across the living room was halfway opened. She tiptoed through the thick, plush carpet and peeked inside. Nikki held her chest in relief when she found Trina lying in bed with a sheet over her naked body. One of Devontae's bodyguards lay snoring beside her in his boxers and socks.

Nikki closed the door and scurried back to the other room.

By the time she finished getting dressed and pinning up her braids, she heard voices looming about. She gulped at the thought of shamefully facing her best friend, who would probably look down at her for cheating on her husband.

The knob to the bathroom door jiggled. "Open the damn door. I gotta piss, man. Shit."

Nikki wasn't surprised that Devontae was acting like a brat as he did the night before. She shook her head and continued applying her makeup. "Hold on!" She took her time even though he wouldn't stop beating on the door. Watching him on television and listening to his songs on the radio hardly conveyed how much of an asshole he really was.

When she opened the bathroom door, Devontae glared at her as if he were going to slap her.

"You all right?" she asked sarcastically. Her smile made him frown even more.

He shoved her out of the way and stood before the toilet. "Hell nah, *bitch*," he spat, looking back at Nikki as he pissed.

She checked out his naked body and smirked at his package, which was smaller than she had envisioned.

Surely smaller than Chance's. She walked away disappointed that what seemed like an opportunity the night before had turned out to be the regret of a lifetime.

"If I say I need to use the bathroom, you need to open the damn door right away, shit. Devontae waits for no one!" A thunderous belch echoed from the restroom.

Nikki ignored him, grabbed her purse, and headed to the living room.

Trina sat on the couch, buckling the strap to her three-inch heels. She looked the other way when Nikki walked in the room.

"Good morning," Nikki said, heading to the refrigerator. She grabbed a bottle of water. Her stomach still felt sour and she doubted that she would feel better by the time she got home. On top of her drowsiness, her back hurt. Maybe Chance would leave her alone if she blamed her hangover on morning sickness. He wouldn't know the difference.

Glancing at Trina, she wondered what was bothering her. "What's wrong?"

Trina lay back on the couch after fiddling with her shoes. "Girl, I got a hangover out of this world!"

"You and me both." Nikki plopped on the couch next to her. "But, I need to hurry home. You know Chance is probably worried about me."

"I know, girl. Let's go. I hope I don't throw up all over the place!"

Nikki helped her friend up, who seemed to still be

tipsy. Trina couldn't even stand straight. They pulled one another along as they bid farewell to the bodyguard.

"Aren't you gonna say goodbye to Devontae?" Trina asked.

Nikki opened the front door and pursed her lips. "Devontae, who?"

❧ ❧ ❧

Quietly closing the door behind her, Nikki looked around. The television loudly played a football game, but Chance wasn't sitting at the couch. Where was he? Her heart skipped a beat when her husband walked into the living room from the kitchen.

"Hey," she said nervously.

"You had fun?"

Nikki gulped. "Yeah. Trina—"

"Yeah," Chance said, sitting on the couch. He grabbed the bowl of popcorn on the coffee table before him. "She already called and told me. How was the concert?"

Nikki smiled as guilt stabbed her all over. Could her sin be seen through her provocative attire? Could he smell the stench of another man on her even though she'd taken a long shower? She fought tears while heading to the bedroom. She stopped when she realized she hadn't answered his question. "It was great."

"You didn't drink, did you?"

She kept walking up the hallway. "No."

She lay in bed and closed her eyes. Maybe when she awoke, everything would have all been a dream.

A knock on the doorframe startled her. "Yes?"

"You okay?" Chance asked, walking into the room.

"Yeah. Morning sickness. That's all."

He sat next to her and stroked her face. "You need me to get you anything?"

Nikki smiled, trying to hide her guilt. "No thanks, sweetie. I need to sleep it off."

Chance stood up. "All right. Well, the fellas are coming by to watch the game."

"Okay. I'll be up by then. I'll make some hot wings or something for you guys. You need me to pick up some beer or something?"

"No. You don't have to make the wings if you're feeling down," he said. "I can have Jeff pick up a pizza with the beer."

Nikki sat up. "Trust me, baby. I've got the wings."

His eyebrows elevated. "You sure?"

She nodded and forced a smile.

Chance kissed Nikki on the forehead. "Thank you, baby." He jumped up and walked to the door. "You know the boys love your wings."

When Chance went back into the living room, Nikki fell back on the bed and sighed.

Chapter Six

C arefully dumping a bowl of sliced potatoes into
bubbling oil, Nikki cradled the phone between
her ear and shoulder.

"I was calling to see how you were doing," she said,
pulling the long phone cord toward her. "I hadn't heard
from you since the concert."

"You know me, girl," Trina replied. "I've been busy
with work, school, church, and the sorority. What are you
doing?"

"Cooking dinner."

"What's on the menu?"

"Nothing special." She grabbed a spatula and pressed
it against the sizzling ground beef. "Burgers and fries.
Wanna come over?"

"Nah. Maybe next time. I've gotten comfortable layin'
in this bed."

Nikki sensed something more. "Is something wrong?"

"Uh-uh. Why?"

"You seem to be upset about something."

"Well…" Trina sighed. "I'm not mad. Just disappointed."

Nikki frowned and stopped flipping the ground chuck patties. "About what?"

"Come on, now," Trina said.

"Don't tell me you're upset about…" Nikki looked around even though she knew Chance wouldn't be home for another ten minutes "…me being with Devontae."

"You're married," Trina reminded her.

"I know. To this day, I don't know what I was thinking." She shook her head, feeling guilty all over again. "I guess in my alcohol-induced state, I reasoned that it was a once-in-a-lifetime opportunity. The man's my favorite singer, for crying out loud! He was all over me!"

"I thought Prince was your favorite singer. You've worn purple every day for the past four years," Trina reminded her.

Nikki pulled a plate from the cabinet. "Well, he *is*. But Devontae came in second. You know that."

"I know, but you act like you're *sooo* in love with Chance. I never thought you would've done something like that."

"Me neither, girl," she said, tearing several paper towels from the roll and covering the plate. "I love Chance with every fiber of my being, and if I could do it all over again, I wouldn't have even gone to the concert, let alone slept with the man." She hovered over the stove. "And if it's any consolation, Devontae's *not* a favorite singer of mine, anymore. All those songs about being a good lover are straight bull! Can't say I'm even a fan."

They both laughed.

"He's so stuck on himself," Nikki continued. "I'm surprised he doesn't rely on *himself* for pleasure."

"I saw that," Trina said, still laughing. "Conceited or not, Devontae can get it! So I really can't blame you. But I would've gotten his number."

"For what? Chance puts it down like no other."

"I heard that."

"But there is something I've been wanting to tell you," Nikki said, pulling a burger from the pan.

"What?" Trina replied eagerly.

Nikki set the burger on top of the plate covered with paper towels. "Girl, I'm finally pregnant," she whispered enthusiastically.

There was silence.

"Hello?"

"Yeah. Girl, that's good," Trina said.

Nikki cocked her head to the side.

"How far are you?"

"I'm not sure yet. I have to go to the doctor."

"Have you told Chance—oh…I forgot. He already thinks you are."

"Yeah. According to him, I'm going on my third month." She pulled the last patty from the pan.

"Mmm-*mmm!*"

❮❮ ❮❮ ❮❮

Chance heard ice clinking against a glass and the slapping of Nikki's flip-flops as she walked through the house from the kitchen. He dropped his pen on his note-book and sighed when she walked in the room with a big smile on her face. A tray sat atop Nikki's palm, balancing a pitcher of lemonade and two glasses.

"Hey."

Chance rubbed his face. He was beyond stressed, and it didn't look like he was going to finish his paper any-time soon. This distraction was guaranteed to set him back another hour.

Nikki placed the tray down on the desk and filled the two empty glasses with lemonade. She handed him a glass as she sipped the other. "How's your studying com-ing along?" She sat on top of the desk, scanning over the law books and papers scattered everywhere.

"Just fine," Chance replied, tight-lipped. He would have been turned on, because she was half-naked in shorts up to her behind with a thin tube-top that only covered her breasts, but sex was the last thing on his mind. "Nikki, I've been needing to ask you something."

Nikki smiled sheepishly.

"Are you sure that you're pregnant?"

She giggled. "Yeah, baby. Why?"

"Aren't you supposed to be like six months or some-thing like that? Why's your stomach still flat?"

Nikki stood up from the desk and poked her stomach out. "Now you know I'm bigger than I was before." She grabbed his hand and placed it on her lower belly. "This is *not* flat."

Sucking his bottom lip, he exhaled through his nose. Chance wanted to believe his wife, but since the last doctor visit, things weren't adding up with him. He knew she was pregnant, because the doctor confirmed it, but something wasn't right.

Nikki kissed him on the cheek. "I'll let you get back to studying." She rubbed her fingers through his curly hair, patted his shoulder, and shut the door behind her.

He stared at the closed door and became lost in thought. Right about now, he was supposed to be in France pursuing his dream as a professional basketball player. Sometimes he felt like he should have gone, anyway. Everyone, except his parents, thought he was a fool to give up a once-in-a-lifetime opportunity for the love of his life. And now, he was beginning to regret it, too.

🐸 🐸 🐸

When Nikki finally gave birth to Rayshad on May 9, 1990, tears poured down her face as she held her son. As beautiful as he was, she knew that Chance was not the father. By then, she couldn't keep her secret any longer. Of course, her husband was the last person she had planned to tell. Trina's mouth dropped open when Nikki revealed the news.

"You lyin'!" she exclaimed, cradling her new godson in her arms.

Nikki wiped away a tear from her eye. "No I'm not."

She sniffed. "Count back to the night of the concert until Rayshad's birthday. The dates match up."

Trina looked down at the baby and shook her head. "Are you sure? Couldn't you have had sex with Chance while you were ovulating? I mean, Rayshad does look kinda like Chance."

"We didn't. He was so stressed out during that time with work and school that he wasn't even in the mood. Majority of the time, I had to ask *him* for it. Besides, Chance and Devontae kinda look alike." She pouted. "Thank God."

Trina rocked Rayshad back and forth. "Are you gonna try to see if it's Devontae's? That's a big child support check, girl!"

Nikki shook her head quickly. "Nah."

"Why not?"

"I've got everything I've ever wanted right here."

Trina sat back on the lumpy couch and smacked her lips.

Even though the walls needed to be painted and the floors were dingy, no matter how much she cleaned them, Nikki knew her job as a housewife well and kept the place immaculate. Their shoestring budget afforded them only the bare necessities, but she never complained, making do with whatever life dealt them. Hand-me-down furniture from his relatives completed their living room and bedroom. She dazzled the sofa and loveseat with couch covers; decorated the scuffed floors with area rugs and runners; and even found expensive-looking artwork from the garment district of downtown L.A.

"Girl, you better wake up!" Trina sucked her teeth. "Come on, now. Be rational. You're not even gonna try to get in touch with Devontae?"

Nikki quickly shook her head.

"Are you gonna tell Chance?"

She looked at Trina like she was crazy. "What do you think?"

🐸 🐸 🐸

Nikki rolled over in bed quietly. Her one-week-old baby seemed to wake up at the sound of a pin dropping. With Chance on the other end of the full-sized mattress, the seemingly long distance between them made her uncomfortable.

She sighed. He had been acting funny ever since Rayshad had been born. If she asked, he always replied as if everything were okay. Didn't take a rocket scientist to know that he was upset about her "year-long" pregnancy. She wondered if he knew the whole truth. A tear fell from her face. Was he curious enough to get a paternity test behind her back?

Nikki faced Rayshad's crib. She was surprised that he wasn't crying. Seemed that was the only thing he did this time of night. With the crib right next to the bed, Nikki thought twice about breaking the silence, but she couldn't take it any longer. "Why won't you talk to me?"

No movement came from Chance's side of the bed. Suddenly, the covers went up and down. "You knew good and well you weren't pregnant before I married you." He sat up and turned toward Nikki.

She gulped.

"Didn't you?"

"Baby, I—"

"Don't lie to me, Nikki." His voice was firm.

"Chance, I was. I'm telling you. I've told you before: I must've had a miscarriage and got pregnant, again. I showed you the pregnancy test."

"Whatever, Nikki." He turned back over and scooted as far to the other side of the bed as possible. "You can get any pregnant woman to pee on a stick."

Chapter Seven

Nine Years Later

Tired from a hard night's work, Nikki dragged upstairs a little past six in the morning. All she wanted to do was fall out, not think about anything, and sleep the day away. Kicking the door to the master bedroom open, her heart sank when she found Chance not there. She dropped everything and darted to her son's room.

No Rayshad.

She held her chest and tried not to panic. What was going on? Maybe Chance had taken Rayshad out for breakfast, but she doubted that highly. Had he walked out on her and taken Rayshad with him? Of course not. Nikki often questioned if Chance even loved Rayshad. The only time he even spoke to him was to scold him and often whipped him for nothing.

"Oh my God." She grabbed the phone and dialed Chance's number. Her heart beat increased with each ring until the voicemail picked up.

"Where are you, Chance?" she screamed into the recording. "And where is my son?" The phone beeped.

She pulled away to see Trina calling on the other line. "You need to call me right away," she demanded before clicking over.

"Hello? Trina?"

"Hey, girl."

"Hey. You're calling early. What's up?"

"Chance didn't tell you?"

"Tell me what?"

"Oh Lord," Trina replied. "I've got Rayshad with me. Chance called me last night and said he had to stay late at the office and asked if I would watch Rayshad."

Nikki was relieved, but shocked that her husband had not told her anything. "Girl, I'm sorry." She grabbed her purse. "I'm on my way, right now."

"It's nothing. Don't worry about it. I'm actually right around the corner. I was calling to see if you had already made it home from work."

Nikki plopped down on the bed and ran her hand through her hair. "Yeah. I'm here."

"What's wrong?" Trina asked.

"Nothing, girl. I was worried about Rayshad. Chance hadn't told me anything."

"Oh, well he's fine," Trina assured her. "I'll be there in a minute."

"All right." Nikki tossed her phone onto the bed. She was so exhausted from working a double shift at the Beverly Hilton that she didn't want to think about anything, but she couldn't help but wonder where her husband was. This wasn't the first time he'd stayed out overnight without telling her, but this was the first time he'd done so while caring for Rayshad.

Standing at the living room window, Nikki watched Trina's green Toyota Camry pull into their driveway a few minutes later. She met them at the front door.

A ten-year-old Rayshad zoomed through the doorway. She stopped him and gave him a big kiss on the forehead. "You have fun with Deon, Tasha, and Auntie Trina?"

He nodded.

"Good. Now, go upstairs and get ready for school."

Trina stepped forward to give Nikki a hug.

"Hey, girl," Nikki said. "Everything okay?"

Trina sighed, following her into the kitchen. "Yeah. Depending on your definition of okay."

"Oh no. What now?" Nikki pulled a bag of coffee from the shelf and prepared the coffeemaker.

Trina sat on a barstool and sighed. "Girl, I don't think I can take it anymore."

Nikki sighed. She had heard that many times before with Trina. She didn't even know why she had married Michael. "Where are the kids?"

"At the daycare already."

"What happened, now?"

Unexpectedly, Trina began to sob. "I'm tired of fighting."

"Aww… I'm sorry." Nikki dropped the coffee filter to rub her friend's back. "He didn't put his hands on you, did he?"

"No. Of course not. I'd be locked up right now, if that

was the case." She spoke nasally. "I'm tired of arguing and him leaving when he feels like it. I can't leave if I wanted to. I've got two kids to take care of."

"Men don't see it that way," Nikki replied, sitting next to Trina. "I go through the same things with Chance."

She sniffed. "Really?"

"Yeah. I stopped crying about it years ago, though. You see how he disappeared last night, had you watch Rayshad, and told me nothing about it."

"Yeah. He was wrong for that. But Nikki, I really think I'm going to go through with it."

Nikki's eyebrows rose. "What?"

"I think I want a divorce." She broke into tears, again. "I can't believe that we've been married for only two years, have two babies, and I'm about to get a divorce!"

Nikki hugged her friend. "It's okay, sweetie. But are you sure you want to get a divorce? You don't want some space and time to think about it first?"

Divorce crossed Nikki's mind every once in a while. Shortly after she had given birth to Rayshad, Chance had become an alcoholic, but even recently she had discovered a small sack of cocaine in his pocket while doing laundry. When she'd confronted him with it, he'd shrugged it off like it was nothing, snatched it from her and finished it off.

Substance abuse was nothing new to Nikki, though. Childhood memories of her mother strung out on drugs reminded her of what she would never do. Even in college when Chance or others offered, she never smoked weed. And even though Chance consumed alcohol daily, she still only drank socially.

There were several nights he didn't come home or would pick arguments as an excuse to leave. And the lack of love he showed Rayshad made Nikki wonder what her husband really knew. Chance never tried to bond with their son, belittled him every chance he got, and only touched him to whip him. According to Chance, Rayshad could do nothing right.

With all things considered, Nikki knew her marriage was not perfect—not by a long shot. But in her world, it was better than most. So, the D-word had never been brought up.

"I've thought about it for a long time, now," Trina replied, wiping her eyes. "Even before I got pregnant with Deon," she sobbed as she referred to her last child. "I'm telling you, girl, I can't take it anymore. I'll kill that man if I stay. He's ruined my entire life!"

"Ruined?"

Trina sobbed. "Look at me. I gave up everything for him. I was born and raised in Beverly Hills. We were the richest family in the neighborhood. Now I'm stuck with a man who barely makes thirty thousand a year."

Nikki had noticed that Trina was not able to buy jewelry and get her hair done every week like she used to. She kept her hair in extension braids for a couple of months at a time to save money and she settled for repeating the same outfits every two weeks.

Tables had turned. Nikki and Chance were living comfortably in their massive-sized Bel Air home. He paid all of the bills and gave her access to all accounts and credit cards. She was able to get anything she desired, including expensive jewelry, designer clothes, and a change in her hairstyle as often as she chose. Working at the Beverly Hilton was something Nikki chose to do to get out of the house.

"It's *that* bad?" she asked, remembering when times were hard in the beginning of her marriage. Because of her own lies, the first two years with Chance were pure hell. But things got better.

Trina nodded. "I can't believe I fell for this! I know I was pregnant with Tasha, but I didn't have to *rush* into it. When he put that ring on my finger, I already knew it wasn't going to work. Hell, I didn't even *love* the man!"

"You didn't?"

Trina shook her head.

Nikki blinked. How could she marry a man she didn't even love?

"See, you're lucky," Trina went on. "You and Chance are living good. Have a nice house. Nice cars. Been married for ten years. I've always wanted that."

"And you still can! Chance and I don't have a perfect relationship. I just haven't given up. Not yet."

"Well, like I said, I can't take it anymore."

Nikki sighed. "Well, do what you have to do. You know whatever it is, I'm there for you. As a matter of fact, you know who to come to if you need representation. Chance has dabbled with divorce before. He'll cut you a deal."

Trina rubbed her nose. "Thank you, girl."

&❧ &❧ &❧

Chance held the door open for Trina and walked outside of the courthouse behind her.

"Thank you," she said, gripping her purse strap.

"No problem."

Jogging down the courthouse steps, Trina looked up at the blue and pink skies above, took a deep breath, and exhaled. She stopped at the bottom step beside Chance and held her hand out. "I really appreciate you, Chance."

He shook her hand. "Ah, you're like family, Trina."

"Seriously," she said, clasping her other hand over their handshake. "I don't know how I would have done this without you." She looked in his eyes. "You really are a lifesaver."

"No big deal. Besides, I might need you to watch Rayshad for me, again. Who knows?"

Trina laughed as they walked up the sidewalk against the busy traffic. Searching through her purse, she said, "I don't know where my checkbook is. Uh! Yes, I do. I left it on the counter at the house. And I know you don't take credit cards."

"Oh, don't worry," Chance said, throwing his hand up. "I know you're good for it. You can pay me another time."

"We can ride by my house and get it now."

"No, really, don't worry about it." They walked into a parking garage. "As a matter of fact, if you need to, you can give it to Nikki, and I'll give you the receipt through her."

"Fair enough," she replied. "But for handling my case in the manner that you did, I really do owe you one, Chance. Why don't we stop at The Palm, and let me get you a drink? I have a couple of dollars on me."

"Are you sure that's a good idea?" he asked.

"What are you talkin' about? You're like my brother-in-law. Besides, I don't like going out alone. And Nikki's on her way to work right about now."

Chance wavered. "I guess a drink or two won't hurt."

"They're on me," Trina replied, pressing her keyless entry button. A green Camry sounded off.

"All right." Chance hopped into his BMW and followed close behind.

🐢 🐢 🐢

Before Chance knew it, he had a strong buzz zinging through his system. From the sounds of Trina's mild slurring, she was past tipsy herself. He knew that it didn't take much for her, though. Back in college during parties or games of Spades, Trina always got drunk off a little of nothing.

Wiping her mouth with a linen after enjoying the

sesame-seared Ahi tuna, she laughed heartily at one of his jokes and took another gulp of her cocktail.

"I've got to thank you again, Chance," Trina slurred. Her eyes were heavy.

Chance's head swayed back and forth. "Nah, nah, nah. How many times do I have to tell you? You're a friend of the family."

"No. I mean it, Chance. This means more to me than you know. Michael took me through it!"

Chance shook his head. "All I did was represent you. No big deal. Any other attorney worth two cents could've done that." He took another gulp of Hennessy. When he put the glass down, Trina gazed at him smiling but looked away bashfully.

Batting her eyes, she looked down at her drink. "You know…" she said, taking a cigarette out of the box.

Chance picked up the lighter beside the ashtray. She leaned forward as he lit the tip for her. "Thank you."

He nodded. "You're welcome."

Exhaling the smoke, Trina looked at him coyly. "You know, it's been about fifteen years?" She counted in space. "I don't know. More or less." She batted her eyes and checked Chance for his reaction. "Does Nikki know?"

Chance's eyebrows rose. He hadn't forgotten about that. That one time. Of course, that was before he ever met Nikki or even knew that she and Trina were best friends. "Not unless you told her," he said.

Trina giggled and tapped the cigarette over the ashtray with her index finger. "I've always envied you two's relationship."

"Nikki and I...we have our problems like all other couples."

She sipped her drink while nodding her head. "Yeah, but you've been strong enough to make things work, though."

"Yeah, well," Chance replied, "as much as I believe in marriage, I don't believe in divorce."

Trina's eyebrows rose.

"I could practice family law and help people get divorced, but criminal defense is more my speed. Why represent something that you don't believe in? And, hell, Nikki and I have our problems, true enough, but nothing that can't be worked out."

Trina huffed. "Is that right?" She shook her head. "You're a good man, Chance."

He smiled. "Thanks...I guess." He looked at his Rolex. "It's almost nine o'clock. We've been in here all evening. It's about that time. We should head out."

"Yeah," Trina replied reluctantly.

Chance opened the book to pay for the tab.

"What are you doing?" She snatched the check out of his hand. "I told you that *I* had this."

"No. I've got this. Don't worry about it."

Trina let go of the receipt and fell back into her seat. She sucked a piece of ice from her cup and stirred her straw around a bit.

After the waiter picked up the check, Chance helped Trina out of her seat. She giggled when the alcohol pushed her back down. As she walked in front of him while they exited the building, he watched her stagger. "Are you sure that you're okay? Do you really think that you're in the position to drive?"

Trina turned around and waved her hand sloppily. "Of course! Why? Do I look—" *Thump!* "Ow!"

Chance turned to find that she had fallen to the ground. He quickly kneeled to help her up. "You okay?"

Trina laughed.

"I think I should follow you home," Chance insisted. "Do you even think you can drive?" he asked again.

Trina was still laughing. "Boy, you know I've got this. But, if you think it would be safe, then yeah, drive me— I mean, follow me home." She hiccupped.

Chance watched Trina carefully as he got into his BMW. While backing out, Trina's Camry pulled out too, almost hitting his car. He drove forward to avoid an accident, and she zoomed off to the edge of the parking lot. He hurried to get behind her, hoping that she wasn't the type of drunk who drove like a bat out of hell.

He was surprised that Trina drove slowly on the way to her apartment, but kept swerving into the opposite lane. Luckily, her apartment wasn't far from the restaurant.

When they pulled up, Chance put the stick in reverse. The car still ran as he waited for Trina to make it inside.

She stumbled out of her car and closed the door shut. As she tried to walk away, she jerked. With her jacket caught in the door, she looked at Chance, laughed, and pointed at another one of her mistakes.

He rolled his window down. "Yeah…you might want to take care of that before you walk off," he replied.

Trina unlocked the door to free herself and turned to Chance. "You should come up for a minute. My checkbook's upstairs and I might as well pay you, now."

Chance looked at the clock. He was already late picking Rayshad up from his parents' home. But, he put the car in park and turned it off. "You sure?" he asked, stepping out. "I can wait until Monday. And then, there's always Nikki."

Trina stepped closely to him and gazed in his eyes. "I insist."

Chapter Eight

T rina stepped into the apartment before Chance, picking up things on the floor as they walked through her unkempt home. "I'm so busy," she explained. "With work and the kids, I don't have time to clean like I need to. Excuse the mess."

"Oh, it's nothing," Chance lied, knowing Trina was making excuses for her junky home. Nikki had a full-time job by choice and still made sure their massive, two-story home stayed spotless. "You actually have a pretty nice place," he fibbed.

A big pile of clothes that she had collected piece by piece blocked her face. "Thank you." Going to a room in the back, she dumped the clothes, pushed something with her foot, and closed the door behind. "Can I get you a drink? Maybe a glass of wine?" She pulled at her lime green blouse to straighten it out.

"Oh *nooo*," Chance sang, waving his hand. "I'm good." He knew he had a higher tolerance, but didn't feel comfortable hanging out at Trina's house. *Just get the check and go.*

"Okay," Trina said glumly. She walked away to get her checkbook. "I don't know why I'm thinking about this," she said, walking back to the front with a pen and her checkbook in hand, "but Nikki promised me that she was going to bake me a carrot cake. She knows how much I love her carrot cakes!"

"I know," he agreed enthusiastically. Things he grew up not to like, Nikki knew how to prepare in ways that made him fall in love. "You see that I've gained quite a few pounds since we've been married." He rubbed his stomach.

She smiled.

His shirt was tucked into his light gray pants with the matching jacket. Two buttons to the pink shirt were loosened, exposing a gold chain lying on his chest.

"I don't care what you say. You still look as good as you did in college. Back when you took us to the championship."

He looked her over and wished he could say the same. Her braids had been in too long, and he probably had seen her in that same outfit several times over the years. Not to mention that she had gained weight after the kids. Her stomach used to be flat, but now spilled over her pants.

She walked in the kitchen, Chance slowly following behind her. "You remember that?" he asked.

Trina pulled two wineglasses from a cabinet and poured wine for the two of them.

He remembered telling her that he didn't want any, but then again, another drink wouldn't hurt. Besides, she only filled the glasses less than halfway.

Trina put her hand on her hip and cradled a wineglass in her other palm. "Of course I remember. You were dating Nikki and I was dating Matt, number seven, at the time." She gulped down her wine.

Chance stood by the table and grabbed his glass. "That's right, Matt Harper." He swallowed his like a shot.

"Mmm-hmm. I remember those days," she said, staring off into space as if she were in a daze. "You and Nikki used to be all over each other. Couldn't pull you two away."

Chance looked distantly. "Yeah." Shaking his thoughts away, he turned back to Trina. "Things change, though." And without realizing it, he started pouring himself another glass.

"Yeah, they do." She stepped close to Chance and looked deeply into his eyes.

He gulped and grew nervous at her bold stare. Looking down, Trina held her empty glass out. He stopped filling his glass to pour hers.

Suddenly, his cell phone rang. He set the bottle down to see who was calling him. It was Nikki. He tucked the phone back into his pocket and picked the bottle back up.

"So, you say that things change," she continued. "How have things changed for you and Nikki? You two don't seem to be as happy as you used to be." She was still standing close to Chance.

He frowned. "Why do you say that?"

"I don't know. I'm going off of how you two used to be in college versus now."

"Hmm." Chance took a sip. "Things *have* changed over the years, and to be honest, I don't know what happened." He downed the majority of his drink. "I should've never gotten married," he mumbled. His eyes widened as he thought twice about what he had said. He shot a look at Trina, who looked surprised herself. "Don't tell Nikki, though. Please don't tell her. I'd never hear the end of it."

"I won't," Trina replied, placing her hand on his shoulder. "You can trust me. We've been friends for what, close to fifteen years now?"

Chance looked down at Trina's hand, which seemed to be very comfortable on his shoulder. When he looked back at her face, she was inching toward him for a kiss. "Wait, wait." He backed away and set his glass of wine down. "You're my wife's best friend."

Trina sighed and swallowed her entire glass. "If I were someone else, would that make a difference?"

Chance didn't respond right away.

"See, Chance, I already know about you. I know how you stay away late nights, sometimes not coming home at all. I know how stressed out you get. How you drink every day. Nikki tells me these things. I tried to tell her long ago that those were signs of an unhappy man. So face it, Chance, you haven't been happy in a long time."

"Yeah, but that doesn't mean I'm going to sleep with my wife's best friend."

"And why not? Is it principle or the fact that you really don't want me?" Before Chance could answer that question, Trina pulled her blouse over her head. He became erect as she tossed her bra to the side, exposing her breasts, which were much bigger than his wife's A-cup. "Be honest."

He blinked, reminded of the first time he had met Nikki in college. Then, that one time with Trina. Acting solely on instinct, he put the glass down and lifted Trina's skirt up. She put her arms around his neck as he took her right there on the kitchen counter.

Chapter Nine

After going over their eleven-year marriage, Chance wondered why Nikki had even thought about coming back into his life seven years later. She sat across in her chair glumly, and even though he felt better about her apologizing, he did not like how their romantic evening turned into an argument.

Nikki's phone started ringing again.

Chance watched her go for the IGNORE button again but grabbed her hand. "Will you take the call?"

"All right." Patting the top of her lip with a linen, Nikki scooted her seat back and avoided eye contact with Chance. Her demeanor was nonchalant as she grabbed her clutch and walked out of listening range.

❧ ❧ ❧

The calm wind blew Nikki's thin purple dress behind her. Long tresses flew high off of her shoulders. Big bright lights across the city and trailing up the strip below glowed harmoniously in the night. She focused on the scenery for a short while before flipping open her phone.

Duncan's number was stored on the voice command feature, but she punched out the digits instead. Explaining herself to him was the last thing she felt like doing on a beautiful night like tonight, but he would keep calling if she didn't say something.

"Where are you?" Duncan said, picking up the phone on the first ring.

Nikki pursed her lips. "Look, an emergency situation happened, and I'm at my mom's right now." She smoothed her palm across a forehead that was now peppered with moisture, knowing that was not the best lie, but it was the only one she could come up with.

"Your mom's?" Duncan hesitated. "Is everything okay?"

"Apparently not." She turned, resting her hip against the railing. Chance was talking to their waiter, but would steal glances in her direction from time to time. "I'm gonna have to talk to you about that later, though. Now's *not* the time."

"Well, something's happened here, too, and I need you to get home."

Nikki let out a weary sigh. "Really? Like what?"

"I've been trying to call you all day to tell you, but as usual, you won't answer."

"Will you tell me what's going on?" Nikki spoke louder than she had intended and Chance's head snapped in her direction.

"Just come clean, Nikki! What are you doing? You're hardly ever home, and it's not like you have a job."

"Excuse me," she shot back. "Being a full-time housewife and mother is a bigger job than you will ever know."

"Yeah, well, you haven't been doing a very good job of either one of them lately."

"Look, I gotta go," Nikki said, pulling the phone from her ear.

"Hold up!" Duncan yelled.

Nikki disconnected the call and dialed her son's number. She didn't feel like being bothered with Duncan and wasn't going to keep Chance waiting too much longer. As the phone rang, she pulled a rainbow palette of eye shadow out of her purse and touched up her makeup; her phone cradled between her ear and shoulder.

"Mother!" Rayshad squealed. "Where are you?"

Nikki couldn't help but laugh at her dramatic son. "Hey, baby. I'm out right now, taking care of some business. Are you okay? Do you need anything?"

"You know I'm fine," he replied as though everything was perfect. "Cooking dinner right now." He lowered his voice and asked, "Did Duncan make you mad?"

Nikki frowned, wondering what he could have overhead that made him think that. "No. Why?"

"Well, really, I should be asking if you made him mad. He's been upset all day. Just threw his phone and broke it a few seconds ago."

"Are you serious?"

"Yeah."

Nikki shook her head. She didn't know that Duncan could even get that upset. "Let me talk to Duncan. Give him the phone."

"Call him on the house phone or something," Rayshad countered smoothly, "because he's *not* getting a hold of *mine*."

Nikki was appalled. Why on earth would Duncan break his phone? Mad or not—that was his business phone— the money line. His clients could reach him any time day or night.

"Where are you?" Rayshad asked.

Nikki sighed. "I've been stressed out lately, so I'm...I need some time alone to get some things together with myself."

"Like what?"

"Well..." Nikki faltered, realizing that she couldn't share anything with her son. He was loyal to her, but he also had a decent relationship with Duncan. She wanted it to stay that way.

"Hold on, Ma. Somebody's clicking over on the other line."

"Call me back later—or I'll call you. I love you, okay?"

"Love you, too, Ma."

A tear slowly coursed down her face, the wetness tickling her cheek. "Bye, baby." She looked out on those colorful lights and somehow they had lost a bit of their sparkle from earlier.

As she walked back over to Chance, she played back their relationship, anger boiling within. There was no way she was going to let him get away with what he'd done. Not this time. Sorry or not.

Chance stood up. "Is everything okay?"

She nodded and swallowed the rest of her champagne. "The show starts in thirty minutes. Let's go."

"Show?"

"Yeah," she said, grabbing her clutch.

"But, I'm ready to gamble!"

Chapter Ten

R ayshad clicked over from Nikki to take the call from his friend Tony, but quickly ended it when he heard, "Lyin' bitch!" He scurried downstairs to see what was going on.

When Duncan looked up from his computer and saw Rayshad staring at him from the doorway of their home office, he quickly changed his demeanor. "Hey! What's up, Rayshad?"

"Nothing." Rayshad's eyebrows elevated. "You all right?"

Duncan crinkled his brow. "Yeah. Trying to get in touch with your mom. Have you heard from her?"

"No," he lied.

"Oh, okay."

Rayshad stepped back into the hallway, but Duncan called for him.

"When was the last time you heard from your father?"

Rayshad's lips parted. *What did that have to do with anything?* "Since they were together. Why?"

Duncan nodded. "Just curious. I'm a little surprised. It's been seven years. That's a long time."

"I haven't lost sleep over it," Rayshad uttered. "How's Demetria?"

"Fine, I guess."

Rayshad walked away on that note. Until Duncan started taking better care of his own daughter, his relationship with Chance was really none of Duncan's business. But he almost felt sorry for his stepfather, who tried best to hide his depression. But Rayshad knew better. After his mother discovered the affair with Marie and the love child, things between Nikki and Duncan had not been the same. And truth be told, he couldn't blame his mom for doing her thing—whatever she was doing and whomever she was doing it with.

Rayshad climbed upstairs, jumped in bed, and stared at the ceiling fan whirling above. He still didn't understand why Duncan wanted to know about the last time he'd seen his father. Truth be told, he couldn't recall the last time, because he was only ten years old when Nikki packed up everything and left. But he did remember that day. The day Nikki left Chance.

🐦 🐦 🐦

Hopping off of the school bus in front of a two-story Bel Air home, Rayshad looked down at his scuffed shoe. "Dang," he mumbled. Now his mother would have to get him a new pair.

When he looked up and scanned the length of the

driveway, he found the back of Nikki's SUV open, filled with luggage. *What's going on?*

Nikki staggered out of the double doors, juggling bags in her hands and under her arms. Rayshad's throat tightened at the sight of the dark red stains on her yellow dress. "Oh my God," he whispered. "Is that blood?"

Nikki inclined her head in the direction of the truck. "Get in, Rayshad. Let's go!"

He shifted his book bag across his shoulder as he rushed toward his mother. Bruises and scratches on her arms and chest became more visible as he approached. "What's happened, Ma?"

Rayshad and Nikki looked up as a drizzle of rain fell onto her face. The sky was dark and gray where they stood, but blue with a hint of sun off into the distance.

Wiping the rain away, Nikki tossed more luggage into the back of the vehicle. Thunder clapped and Rayshad scurried into the passenger seat so his hair and clothes wouldn't get wet. He slammed the door and took a look at the backseat, amazed at the amount of boxes and suitcases blocking his view of the back window.

Nikki quickly hopped into the driver's seat, started the engine, put it in reverse, and slammed her foot on the gas before tearing out of the driveway like a maniac.

He gripped the dashboard. "What happened, Ma? Did Chance—?"

"Just be quiet right now, all right?"

Within seconds, rain poured from the sky. She clicked

the windshield wipers on high, but the roadway in front of them was barely visible.

"We're going to a friend's house," she said, slowing down to a safer speed.

"Trina?" he asked.

"No. You'll see when we get there." The sweat on her face and smeared makeup told a story that he was eager to find out. He was tempted to say something else, but instead focused on the drops of rain dancing on the passenger window.

Rayshad never really understood his mother and father's relationship. They bickered a lot over the smallest things, but always kissed and made up. And not once had their fights ever gotten physical. Chance often reminded Rayshad that a man should never put his hands on a woman, but something crazy had happened back at their home in Bel Air. And, he was going to find out what.

When his mother shook him awake an hour later, he stretched and looked out of the window at a condo on Redondo Beach. "Where are we?"

Nikki's eyes were still red and she looked as frazzled as she did when he had gotten home from school. "I already told you: a friend."

Rayshad followed his mother on a concrete trail in the middle of the sand, watching the blue ocean waves crash along the beach. While they climbed up the steps, a door swung open without a knock.

A tall, dark man with a shiny bald head stepped outside and gasped. "Oh my God." His wide eyes traced the blood sprayed on Nikki's yellow dress. "What the hell happened? Who did this to you?"

Nikki looked down at Rayshad. "I'll tell you later."

Rayshad studied the muscular man who had one of the deepest voices he had ever heard. The tall man bent over and held his hand out. "Hey, man."

Rayshad looked up at his mother before shaking it. "Hey."

"What's your name?"

"Nikolas. But everyone calls me Rayshad."

"Good to meet you, Rayshad. I'm Duncan, a friend of your mom's. We grew up together."

Rayshad nodded.

"You guys come inside."

🐱 🐱 🐱

A week after they had stayed over Duncan Johnson's house, Rayshad caught hold to his mother's silk robe, demanding to know, "How long are we gonna be here?"

Nikki sat back down on Rayshad's bed, rubbed his curly hair, and pulled the blanket over him. It smelled like flowers and fabric softener.

"When are we going back home?" he asked, looking over her nightgown and robe.

Nikki pressed a hand to his cheek, then leaned in to kiss the tip of his nose. "We're not," she replied candidly.

Even though he could barely see her in the darkness, he understood the side-to-side motion of her head.

"How come?"

She sighed wearily. "Well, Chance and I are in the middle of making a few decisions right now."

"Are you getting a divorce?"

Nikki flinched, but didn't answer right away. She pulled the covers up to his neck and whispered, "We'll talk about all of that later. Okay, baby? You've got school in the morning." She tucked him in tightly.

"I know."

Nikki kissed him one last time, then walked toward the door.

"Ma?"

She turned to face him, the window above his bed shining down on her to a point he could see her tear-stained face.

"I hope you *do* get a divorce."

Nikki pressed her hand against her chest. "Why would you say something like that?"

"I don't like Chance."

She made her way back to the bed and perched on a spot near him. "Why?"

"Because…" Rayshad rubbed his eye. "He's so mean to me. I wish he wasn't my father. I wish Duncan was my father."

Nikki stroked his hair continuously but did not say anything.

He hoped that she would tell him what he wanted to hear, but instead she stood up and said, "Lay back down." Nikki stepped into the hallway and grabbed the doorknob. "Close your eyes," she said softly, "and go to sleep."

But, sleep took the longest time to come.

Chapter Eleven

Duncan held his hands over Nikki's eyes, shifting her forward along the way. He held her close, enjoying the scent of her perfume. Smelled like the new one he had bought her a couple of weeks ago.

"Keep them closed," he said, feeling her lashes flutter between his fingers.

"How much more do we have to go?"

Duncan guided her a few more steps. "Okay. You can open them now."

After he dropped his hands from her face, she gasped for air. She stood in the middle of a large, empty living room with high ceilings. From her reaction, he knew that this house was ten times better than the house she and Chance had in Bel Air. She stepped to the side, spread her arms out, and turned in circles like a little kid on a playground.

Duncan beamed, trying to keep up with her frantic movements. "What do you think?"

Nikki skipped toward her husband and jumped in his arms. "I love it!" Her voice echoed through the empty mansion.

"I got it for a steal," he said, kissing her forehead as he lowered her to the ground. "I'm pretty cool with the guy, and he owed me a few favors anyway."

"Oh my God!" Nikki squealed. "First, the wedding, now this!" She jumped into his arms again and planted a kiss on his lips, then stepped into the adjoining dining room. "I enjoyed the view of the water at your condo but I mean, Beverly Hills?"

"You deserve it, Nikki. From the time we met back in high school, I knew you were the one. When you went away to college, I thought I'd never see you again, but when I bumped into you a few months back, I swore I'd never let you go." He still couldn't believe that he had found her behind the front desk of the Beverly Hilton seven months earlier.

As he approached the front desk toting a laptop bag, he asked himself, "Is that Nikki Carter?"

Nikki looked up from the computer screen and blinked twice. "Duncan?" Her mouth dropped when she was certain that it was him.

They laughed and she walked around the counter to give him a hug.

Duncan set his bag down and embraced his long-lost friend. "Oh my God, Nikki. What a small world!" Duncan looked her over and couldn't believe that she was even more beautiful now than before. "You look great!"

She put her hands on her hips and looked him up and down. "So do you."

He couldn't stop smiling. "How's life been treating you?"

"It's been good."

"And your mom?" she inquired. "How's Mrs. Johnson?"

"Oh. She passed away a couple of years ago," he said quietly.

"No!" Nikki whispered.

"She used to ask about you or bring you up every now and then."

"Really?" He could never forget that smile.

Duncan remembered when a seventeen-year-old Nikki had moved in with them for a couple of months during a time she had nowhere else to go. After that summer, she had gone off to begin her freshman year at UCLA and never returned. He knew even then that women as beautiful as her didn't stay on the market too long and he wasn't surprised when she had stopped calling.

Duncan parted his lips to ask Nikki about her mother but knew that topic was a bit too sensitive for now. He had often wondered if her mother was still in jail.

Nikki walked back behind the front desk. "Do you have a reservation?"

"Yeah. Duncan Johnson."

She turned to the computer and began typing.

"How long has it been?" he asked, looking up. "About fifteen years?"

She nodded. "Wow. Time flies."

Duncan had been so busy building an empire that he hadn't had time to commit to anyone seriously. But seeing his first love again, made him rethink the possibility of getting married and maybe even having children.

But the big rock on her finger said it all. How could he have missed it as he watched her slender, manicured fingers type in the information to pull up his reservation?

"So you've gotten married?" he asked. "Have any kids?"

Nikki blushed. "Yes. We've been married for almost ten years now. And I have a son. He's nine. What about you?"

"Single, no kids."

She frowned. "Really? Why?"

"Just hadn't found the one."

Nikki nodded.

"But I hope it wouldn't be a problem if I wanted to take you out for lunch. Something completely innocent. We've got a lot to catch up on."

"That's fine, we can go out as *friends*," she said in a voice laced with a confidence only a self-assured woman could have.

Duncan gazed into her light brown eyes, but she looked away too soon. He grabbed her hand, relishing how soft it was as he bowed and kissed it delicately. "Friends it is."

What luck would have it that Nikki separated from her husband only a couple of months later, when her best friend confessed to an ongoing affair with Chance? Chills traveled through his body when he saw the dark bruises and red scratches on Nikki's arms and chest, but after she had described the physical altercation she'd had with Trina, Duncan was confident that the feisty Nikki he knew back in high school had given Trina what she had coming to her.

Nikki was really hurt behind their affair, but when Trina died in a fatal car wreck a few months later, Nikki expressed regrets of letting go of their friendship. Every day, she filled his ears with her troubles and he gave her a shoulder to cry on. Duncan understood that she needed her space and time to heal, so he didn't put his own desires on her. But the night her divorce was finalized, she quietly stepped into his bedroom and locked the door. Her silk robe fell to the floor and she crawled on top of him.

Two months later, he proposed.

Duncan never spoiled any other woman of his past. Dinner dates was as much as he had given, but after finding out Nikki had eloped for her first marriage, he provided her with a grand ceremony of her dreams. Even though the only people she knew in the huge audience was mostly Duncan's family, his acquaintances, and her ex-co-workers from the Beverly Hilton, she cried at the lengths Duncan had taken to see her happy.

As Nikki ran up and down the halls of the empty mansion, Duncan gave her ideas to decorate their new home. "George is friends with an interior designer who works with A-list celebrities and can have this place looking like a page out of a magazine," he said, scanning the length of the master bedroom closet. "I also know a guy who owns a housekeeping service."

"Are you crazy?" Nikki said, her hand riding up her hip. "Leave all that to me. Now that I don't have to punch a clock anymore, I'm going back to doing what I do best: being a housewife." She kissed Duncan on the lips. "Even being the best lover in the world comes second to my cooking."

Duncan hugged her close and planted another round of kisses. "Your cooking's good, but I'm going to have to argue with you on that one."

Nikki stepped into the chef's kitchen that was begging for her to do some damage. "That's one argument you might lose."

Chapter Twelve

Waking to the sound of birds chirping often brought a smile to Nikki's face. Six years into her marriage with Duncan, she still got up before anyone else—even before the sun.

Wrapped in a silk oriental robe, she strolled downstairs to the sweet aroma of French Roast coffee brewing in the automated coffeemaker. The kitchen was her favorite room, not only because she loved to cook, but she had it remodeled to her specifications before they moved in. Newly installed cabinets, countertops, and floors complemented her favorite stainless steel appliances.

Oil paintings of wine bottles, vineyards and grapes adorned the walls, and a crystal vase filled with fresh flowers that Nikki snipped from her garden daily sat on top of the breakfast table. While the sunrise slowly poured its light through the sheer curtains, she sipped a hot cup of coffee and relished the peaceful turn that her life had taken.

What to cook? Nikki thought as she finally headed to the refrigerator. She had to think of something creative when it came to preparing meals, so no one would ever complain that her food was boring. The kitchen bookshelf was filled with recipe books and master chef DVDs, most of which Nikki had memorized and altered according to the family's taste. A flat-screen television had been built into the west wall, so she could watch cooking shows as she prepared her next masterpiece.

She opened the refrigerator to study the assortment of foods: organic vegetables, fruit, and beverages. The *Today* show kept her company on the television as she went about preparing shrimp omelets.

Duncan stepped into the kitchen thirty minutes later wearing the suit Nikki had laid out for him, coordinated with tie, pin, cufflinks, watch, socks, and shoes. She could smell the Versace cologne that she had pulled to the forefront of the other bottles lined up on the dresser. Before they got married, all he ever wore was a white dress shirt with slacks. And, soap was his cologne.

"Good morning." Nikki stepped forward and kissed her husband. After wiping her damp hands on her black apron, she fixed his tie and asked, "How did you sleep last night?"

"All right." He looked into her eyes, grinning as he teased, "Especially after how you put it on me last night, this morning…"

She gave him a playful slap on the behind.

"See, you did some of that too. What am I going to do with you?" He leaned down to kiss her, again. "I've got a lot of things to do today, but need to prepare for that business trip to Ontario. You'll pack for me?"

"Sure." Nikki's smile hid how she truly felt about her husband's business trips. After all, that was how she had met up with him six years ago. But she trusted Duncan. A lot more than she did Chance. And as long as he continued to take care of her and Rayshad, she wasn't going to complain about a thing.

Rayshad ambled into the room wearing a green sweater and stone-washed jeans that hugged his lean frame. His shoulder-length curly hair was smoothed back into a ponytail. "Hey." He planted a kiss on his mother's cheek and sat down where a plate was already set out for him.

She beamed. "Good morning."

Duncan took a seat across from Rayshad and popped open the *USA Today*.

Nikki turned to find her son frowning at his plate as though maggots were crawling on his eggs.

Nikki shook her head. "Eggs, too?"

"Ma, they come from chickens," he said in a tone that meant she should know better.

She pulled Rayshad's plate from the table, dumped the omelet, and placed it back before him. "Happy, now?" Only French toast and hash browns remained.

Rayshad smiled pleasantly. "Charmed, but could you slice me a grapefruit and sprinkle a little sugar on top? Thanks."

Nikki dismissed him with a wave, but grabbed a large,

yellow grapefruit from the fruit bowl and prepared it for him. "Did you sleep well?"

"Not really. I'm beginning to think I need a new mattress," he said, rubbing his side. "It's got a lump in it from me laying in the same spot all the time."

Nikki set the small plate of grapefruit before him.

"Oh, really? Why didn't you tell me that before?" She returned to the counter and took a sip of her coffee, stealing glances at the morning news.

"Don't worry about it," Duncan said, folding the newspaper until he reached the business section. "You think you have the time to go pick one out and have it delivered by tonight?"

She walked toward the table and removed the parts of the paper that never mattered to him. "Of course." She stroked a hand on Rayshad's face. "Anything for my little prince."

"Little?" He pulled away from her touch. "I'm sixteen years old."

"Of course," she said. "For my *man*."

"And get the best one they've got," Duncan added, bristling at the term she used to describe her son. "Use the Black Card. I just paid the balance off."

"Oh, and I'm bringing a friend by on Thanksgiving," Rayshad tossed in.

"Friend?" Nikki looked from her son to Duncan.

Duncan's eyebrows rose.

Rayshad didn't have many friends—at least not of the

opposite sex. Was he finally making a few after all this time?

"Friend, like girlfriend, friend?" Duncan queried.

Nikki's golden skin turned bright red as she beamed at her son, but said to her husband, "Yes, he means girl-friend!"

Rayshad rolled his eyes. *"Ma…"* he whined. "A friend, okay?"

"Oh okay." Nikki tried to hide her excitement behind a sip of coffee, and Duncan purposefully hid behind the newspaper to avoid her "I told you so" glare.

A couple of years back, Duncan and Nikki had the biggest argument when he had questioned Rayshad's effeminate ways.

"My son's *not* gay, all right?" she had snapped one night in bed. "He's a little…" Nikki searched for the word… *"proper*, and maybe a little soft, but that's because he's spent all of his life up under me." She pulled the Sorrento Italian bedspread over her. "It's bad enough that I have to deal with the kids taunting him at school."

Duncan said nothing more, but Nikki felt obligated to keep going.

"He's church-going," she reasoned. "He goes to church more than me and you, for crying out loud. I think I've raised a good boy."

Duncan tilted his head in her direction. "Yeah, well, he's *good*, but it would be nice to see him interested in women at some point."

"I can't believe..." Nikki stood up and yanked the comforter off of the bed.

"What are—"

She stormed out of the room leaving him with only pillows and sheets.

Since that night, Duncan never spoke about her son that way again, but his body language always gave himself away.

She tried to make eye contact with him, but he stayed sheltered behind the newspaper. *Coward!*

Nikki had held those same sentiments about her son for years, but it was hard hearing it voiced by someone else.

She remembered the days Rayshad came running home crying because the kids at school made fun of him. Chance was quick to knock the boy upside his head for not holding his ground like a man. Nikki always came to his defense, pressing Rayshad against her bosom.

"Quit treating him like a baby!" Chance spat.

"Whatever, Chance. He's just a child."

Rayshad's dark curly hair, golden skin, beautiful face and proper ways often made him a target for bullies. When Nikki had decided to confront the bullies herself, Rayshad had come home days later with a black eye, discouraged more than before, whining that she only had made things worse.

Growing older, his tears dried and he stopped expressing his feelings to Nikki. But one day, out of nowhere, he had asked his mother, "What is it about me that makes people think I'm gay?"

Nikki had cringed and tried to hold back her tears. Children could be so cruel. Rubbing a hand softly across the side of his face, she had replied, "I don't know. Because I don't see it."

Deep down, she knew that her son had a "way" about him, but that didn't necessarily mean he was gay. She figured that with time he would grow out of it and become more masculine. And if he didn't, so what? Her favorite singer Prince wasn't gay, and he was as smooth and graceful as he wanted to be.

"They say that because you look good, and they're intimidated by that. That's all." She rubbed his curly hair and pulled him close.

As the years grew, so did his confidence. After visiting the gym regularly to lift weights, he acquired a lean, athletic build that turned heads everywhere he went. Rayshad knew he was fine, and there was no one who could tell him otherwise. Even though some people still questioned his sexuality, there were always young ladies who found him very attractive; especially after he received a new Ford Mustang for his sixteenth birthday. She was happy to see that he was enjoying life and thoughts of what he may or may not be were put on the back burner. But every now and then she would notice Duncan peering at her son as though he was trying to figure him out. Only then did a sliver of doubt creep in. At least Duncan didn't deal with it the way that Chance had. But his silence was as hurtful as if he'd landed a blow.

Nikki poured more coffee in Duncan's cup. "Well, I'm

excited to meet your new friend," she said to Rayshad. "What's her name?" She knew he had not specified that he was inviting a female, but she had high hopes. Duncan peeked around the paper to take in the answer.

"Carissa," Rayshad replied in a tone that said he was tired of the exchange.

Nikki's heart soared. "Ah. Carissa…what a pretty name."

She looked over in Duncan's direction to see that he had taken a sudden interest in rereading the same section he had finished five minutes ago.

The phone rang and Rayshad stood as though he was going to answer, but switched directions and headed toward the door. "I'm late for school. See you guys later."

Nikki reached for the phone and removed it from the cradle.

"I need to get out of here, as well," Duncan said, folding the newspaper and strolling over to give her a kiss. He made his exit behind Rayshad.

Nikki fumbled with the cordless phone as it rang a third time. She did not recognize the number on the caller ID, but answered anyway.

"Hello?"

"Nikki?"

Nikki froze. "Hel-lo…" she whispered, trying to decipher the voice with that one word. Suddenly, it hit her. Everything within tensed as she stumbled toward the breakfast table, slipped into the chair Rayshad had vacated, and took a deep breath. Twenty years had passed since she had last spoken with the woman on the other end.

Chapter Thirteen

Nikki's hands and voice trembled as she ground out a single word…"Ma?"

"Oh…Nikki!" Gina Carter gushed. "I can't believe you recognize my voice after all these years!"

Nikki closed her eyes and tried not to think of all the things she had gone through so many years ago. But how could she forget? Gina's disappearances. The drugs. But more than anything—the murder.

"Hello?"

Nikki sighed. "Yeah, I'm here." She looked at the dishwasher, but was too distracted to do anything but hold her ground at the kitchen table.

"So…are you excited to hear from me?"

Nikki choked back her original thought and said, "I…I…I don't know if excited's the right word. I'm…surprised."

Gina cleared her throat. "After all these years, that's what you've got to say to me?"

What did she expect? "There are a lot of things I have to say to you, but I don't know how."

"Excuse me, young lady?"

"Young? Ma, I'm thirty-seven years old. And, all I'm saying is: how do you expect me to be excited after what happened the last time I saw you?"

"That was twenty years ago, Nikki," Gina snapped. "All that's in the past, now."

"Twenty years ago? Funny, I remember things like they were yesterday. As much as I *try* to keep them in the past, they don't go away."

"You need to lower your voice, I know that."

"I always thought it was funny how you would disappear for months at a time, leaving us to fend for ourselves, and then come back bossing us around like you had the right."

"I did then, and I still do now. Mistakes or not, I'm still your mother."

Nikki stood up. "Yeah, well, I'm not a child anymore. Because of you, I haven't been a child since I was ten."

"See, now you're making things up. I'm not about to sit here and listen to this nonsense when I know I did all I could."

"All you could?" Nikki stopped herself from snapping like she really wanted to. "We had to learn how to survive on our own. If anyone was a mother in our household, it was *me!*" There was a moment of silence.

"Nikki, I know I've made many mistakes in the past. And I'm sorry. I really am."

Nikki held her breath to hear the first apology that ever came from her mother's lips. Even though it didn't wipe away the pain, that alone was worth listening to.

"Well…" Nikki said, in a calmer tone. "I'm sorry for getting mad just then."

Gina sighed as if *she* had the right to be upset. Nikki could only shake her head.

"And to be quite honest, I *am* glad that you called."

"You are?" Gina said as if she were shocked. "I couldn't tell. You didn't come visit me once."

Nikki frowned. "Answer me something, Ma." Her tone was sharp. "Why on earth would I want to come see you after what I went through?"

"I still deserved to see you. For twenty years, I sat up lonely wondering what was going on in your life."

"Well, for *ten* years, I sat around waiting on you, wondering if you were ever going to come home for good. When were you going to stop doing the drugs? Or thought maybe you weren't going to ever come home, because you dropped dead from an overdose! Those were the things that went through my head every day while you were out in the streets. Who do you think took care of Latrice when you were gone?"

Gina remained silent on the other end.

"So, why are you calling now?" She tapped her foot, wanting to end the call, but hanging up would be rude. "I hope you don't need anything. I hope the twenty years you spent in jail was enough time for you to kick your addiction."

"I don't want anything from you!" Gina yelled. "I was

calling to apologize and ask for your forgiveness! But with all this disrespect, I don't even want *that!*"

Nikki let out a long, slow breath. "Look, Ma. I'm sorry. Okay? I'm glad you called." No matter how angry she was with her mother, curiosity kicked in. "Thanksgiving is in a couple of days." She gathered the dirty plates on the table. "Why don't you come by for a visit? I'm cooking dinner."

Gina was silent so long Nikki thought the call had dropped. Suddenly there was a soft, "Are you sure?"

"Yes. I would love to see you."

Chapter Fourteen

Thanksgiving Day arrived in a flurry of activity even though the only two guests invited were Nikki's mother and Rayshad's friend. After scrubbing the entire mansion down, Nikki slaved in the kitchen for two days preparing a meal fit for a king: smoked turkey, glazed ham, dressing, mashed potatoes, gravy, yams, green bean casserole, asparagus, macaroni and cheese, deviled eggs, seven-layer salad, and cranberry sauce. She wasn't sure what kind of pies her guests liked, so she made several—pecan, sweet potato, pumpkin, and apple. She almost didn't make peach cobbler, but remembered from childhood that her mother loved it. Carrot, red velvet, and German chocolate cakes were also on the dessert menu.

"Will you calm down?" Duncan pleaded, as Nikki pulled golden brown rolls from one of the ovens. "It's just your mother."

"I know, but…" Nikki tossed the oven mitt in a drawer and leaned against the counter. She tried to explain the situation to Duncan before, but he still didn't seem to understand. "I don't want to get into an argument with her."

Duncan wrapped his arms around her. "I know."

"I haven't seen her in such a long time that I don't even know what to expect. And you know I don't like surprises. I hate the unexpected."

The doorbell rang.

Instead of making a break for it, Nikki reached up and adjusted his collar.

Duncan grabbed her fidgeting hands. "Everything will be fine."

Although they had dated for two years in high school and she had been close enough with his family to move in after the murder, Nikki never had unveiled all of the things she had gone through growing up. All he knew at that time was that Gina had killed her own boyfriend and gone to jail for it. He didn't understand what it was like to be forced into maturity at an early age and go through any means necessary to survive. Both of his parents had raised him in a safe, middle-class community, which was a far cry from the malicious ghetto Nikki had come from.

After hearing from Gina for the first time in twenty years, Nikki woke up sweating from the first nightmare she'd had in years. Feelings she buried away for so long began to resurface and she questioned whether seeing her mother again after all of these years was such a good idea.

"Stop worrying so much," Duncan said, holding her

sweaty palm. "She'll probably be proud, like any other mother, that her daughter married a successful man. Does she remember me?"

"I didn't tell her that we had gotten married. I'm sure she does, though." Duncan was her first and only boyfriend in high school.

The doorbell rang again.

"Come on, let's answer it." He wrapped his arm around her waist as the heels of their shoes clicked against the marble floors of the hallway. "You're over-analyzing things as usual."

Nikki bought more time when she stepped into the living room, fluffing pillows on the couch and tinkering with a flower arrangement. Then she stood before a mirror near the front door, pulling at her curls. She smoothed a manicured hand across her orange dress and checked her overall look.

"Will you open the door already?" Duncan said.

Nikki's hand trembled as she reached for the door handle. She closed her eyes and swung the door open.

"Nikki?" said a raspy voice. Gina cleared her throat.

She slowly peeled her eyes open and cupped her hand over her mouth. "Oh my God," she said, fighting tears. A glimpse of a younger Gina strung out on drugs flowed into her memory, then it transformed into the frighteningly skinny, fragile and drawn woman who stood before her.

Gina's thin lips curled into a smile and she released a

gleeful laugh. "Ha-Ha! Come here, girl!" Holding her arms open, she stepped forward.

Lost in her thoughts of the past, Nikki froze. She remembered the beauty that her mother once had and Gina looking too innocent to have ever been caught up in a lifestyle that would lead to jail. Nikki broke down and cried like a baby.

Gina gripped her daughter tightly for a long time.

Nikki pulled away and looked at her mother's wrinkled face. The whites of her swollen, tired eyes were gray and her sagging, brown skin had thousands of angular lines stretching across her full face. Gina was only in her mid-fifties, but looked like she was approaching one hundred.

She had witnessed firsthand the hard life Gina had lived, but would have never imagined that she could look so close to death. Maybe it was the drugs. They did do horrible things to people who couldn't shake their habits. Maybe it was her time in prison. Probably a combination of both.

"Hey, baby," Gina said, wiping away tears of her own. The smile that broke across those thin, brown lips only brought more tears to Nikki's eyes.

When Nikki stepped back and took another full-sized view of her mother, she started crying again. "You look beautiful." She sniffed and couldn't stop staring through the tears.

"Thank you." Gina leaned to the side and looked past Nikki. "Are you going to let me in?"

"Oh!" Nikki wiped her face and moved aside. "Please, come in."

Gina stepped forward and smiled at Duncan who stood off to the side allowing the women time to reconnect.

"It's so nice to see you, again, after all these years!" Duncan opened his arms wide.

Gina reluctantly accepted the hug. "Hey. And you are?"

Nikki should have known Gina wouldn't have recognized Duncan. "He's my husband. I thought you would have remembered Duncan."

"Oh."

"Duncan and I went to high school together. He took me to prom." Nikki remembered Gina being around for her senior prom in rare form back then—sober. She was even there to see her graduate from high school. But from Nikki's tenth to sixteenth birthday, Gina had been constantly in and out of her daughters' lives.

"Oh, okay," Gina said as if though she still didn't recognize him. "Yeah," she went on, "I pulled up to this neighborhood of big mansions and said, 'This *can't* be where Nikki stays.'"

Nikki gave Gina's faded, shapeless turquoise dress a quick once-over.

"You've come a long way, girl!"

Nikki forced a laugh.

Gina patted Duncan on the back. "You must be the billionaire."

Duncan laughed, his eyes twinkling with warmth. "Not billion, but I'm working on it."

"Hmm, too rich for my blood," Gina quipped. "You know, we can all share the wealth."

Nikki's eyes widened at her mother's bluntness and quickly led her to the dining room table before she could let another one of her "jokes" loose.

"You look really nice," Nikki said, following behind her mother who walked slowly with a limp.

"Why, thank you."

"I would give you the *grand tour*," she went on, "but I don't want the food to get cold."

"*Grand tour?*" Gina turned around and looked up at her daughter, who was several inches taller than her. "There's more?" She sucked her teeth and blinked twice at something behind Nikki. "And what's with this big old Christmas tree? Christmas is a month away! I pulled up, saw the decorations outside and thought I forgot to bring gifts."

"I got an early start," Nikki replied, turning her mother back around to guide her to her seat. "People usually start decorating the day after Thanksgiving."

"You don't say."

Nikki headed to her seat at the end of the table, but Gina plopped down in her spot. Duncan held up a hand to keep her from bringing that to her mother's attention. She sat down next to Duncan, miffed about her displacement.

The older woman looked around, staring at the beautiful watercolors in antique golden frames, which clung to off-white, paisley-printed wallpaper. Colorful plants in the finest flowerpots were strategically placed in every corner of the room. A built-in China cabinet with mirrors and lights displayed a collection of exotic vases from all over the world. "Your house is nice, though. Came pretty far from where we're from."

"Thank you."

"Now, where's my grandson, Raymond?"

Nikki cleared her throat. "It's Ray*shad*."

"Yeah, I know," Gina replied, flicking her as though dismissing the correction. "I'm not that old. But it does sound like a girl's name to me." A stab of pain entered Nikki's heart.

Duncan tried to fight a smile and avoided eye contact with his wife.

Gina continued, but Nikki found it hard to focus. She shook her head, trying not to criticize everything her mother said or did. For a moment, she wondered if her mother had hit the pipe before coming over. But then again, Nikki could hardly remember her mother's sober personality, so that wasn't much she could use for comparison.

"To be honest, I don't know where he is," Nikki replied. "He's usually home around this time. He *never* misses dinner. Said he was bringing a friend, too."

"Well, the food looks delicious!" she exclaimed, snatching a roll from the basket and tearing into it as though she hadn't eaten a meal in ages. "Had it catered? No. Let me guess. With a house like this, you probably have a live-in cook." Gina looked at Duncan and laughed.

He stood up on cue. "Would you like me to fix you a plate?"

Nikki tried not to be offended a third time and gulped her wine before saying, "No, I cooked."

"Oh. I don't remember teaching you how to cook." Gina handed her plate to Duncan.

"I used to cook all of the time," Nikki said flatly, shifting in her seat. "Maybe you don't remember, but I was the only person in the house who cooked for a long time."

Duncan reached across her and spooned a heap of potatoes on the plate.

Gina pursed her lips. "Yeah, well…" She chomped half of a roll into her mouth. "It's good."

Nikki waited for Duncan to finish fixing their plates. "Shall we say grace?" She reached for Duncan's hand and bowed her head.

As he went forth with prayer, Gina chewed her food loudly and took a good look around. Nikki watched her from a half-opened eye and cringed when her mother picked up the china and looked at the sketching on the underside. Then, she grabbed her wineglass and gulped sloppily, leaving red spots on her dress and the tablecloth.

"…Amen," Duncan ended.

"Amen," Nikki and Gina echoed.

"You know, I didn't mean to talk about your son's name like that," Gina said to Duncan. "I probably said something to offend you as a father, and if I did—"

Duncan shook his head, holding his hand up to ward off the apology that was certain to follow. "No need."

"Hmm."

"Ma," Nikki interjected, "Rayshad is Duncan's stepson. I had Rayshad in a previous marriage."

Gina's head went up. "Oh, really?"

"Yeah."

"We have a lot to catch up on, then. And speaking of previous…um, what's up with all of that?"

Nikki followed her mother's gaze to the cleavage-revealing dress she wore.

"They don't make them that size in my family. And they weren't anywhere that big when you were a teenager."

Duncan nearly choked on a deviled egg.

"Would you like some more sparkling grape juice, Ma?"

"Juice? No wonder that stuff was so sweet." Gina looked at Duncan's and Nikki's glasses. "Is that what you two are drinking?"

"Well—"

"Yes," Duncan quickly said. He eyed Nikki, as if he wanted her to agree and stood to refill Gina's glass with sparkling grape juice.

"What are we toasting to?" Duncan asked casually.

She held her glass up. "Toasting to this reunion with my mother. It's a blessing that you are here with us this Thanksgiving. *Truly* a blessing that you're back in my life."

Gina smiled and took a big gulp.

They ate quietly for a short while with Duncan looking at Gina and sometimes shifting his gaze toward Nikki, as though wondering when either one of them were going to say something.

Nikki broke the silence. "So where do you stay?"

"Not too far from our old house," Gina replied. "It's a small apartment. Perfect for me."

Nikki didn't like the sound of that. The old neighborhood they used to stay in was in horrible condition back then in the eighties and had never been rehabilitated. "You know, that's not the safest neighborhood," Nikki said, taking in a forkful of dressing.

"Oh, I know it's not. But, you only think that now because you're living up here in the hills like a movie star. Don't forget that you were just staying there not too long ago, yourself."

Nikki wanted to forget. Who wanted to hold on to painful memories?

A door shut in another room.

Everyone looked up and Nikki smiled when Rayshad entered dressed in a black coat and dress pants. Nikki beamed at her son, pleased that today he wore his long curly hair out. He looked much like Chico DeBarge with that hairstyle and preferred it over his usual ponytail.

A petite, young woman with a slender but athletic build walked in behind him.

Nikki stood and gave Rayshad a kiss. "Hey, baby."

"Hey, Ma. Duncan." He eyed Gina and nodded his head. "This is my friend, Carissa Hudson."

Nikki's smile widened. "Carissa, that's a pretty name."

Like the extensive wardrobe in his closet, Rayshad seemed to have good taste in women. Carissa had hair that touched just above her waist, olive skin, big gray eyes, a classically pert nose, and full pink lips.

Carissa clasped her hands and lowered her gaze. "Thank you."

"It's nice to meet you, Carissa," Nikki said, standing up. "Please, join us for dinner."

"Nice to meet you, too." Her soft voice was barely louder than a whisper.

Rayshad helped his friend take off her gray pea coat and pulled out her chair. She took a seat, holding the back of her skirt to her thighs.

Nikki eyed Gina who, between stuffing her mouth with food, was looking Rayshad up and down. "Rayshad, I want to introduce you to my...my mother."

He blinked. "*Your* mother? You mean, Duncan's mother?"

Nikki smiled nervously. "No. This is *my* mother, Gina Carter."

Rayshad's stunned expression said a lot. Nikki had some explaining to do. When he was a curious five-year-old, asking where her mother was, Nikki had told him that she didn't have one.

"Well..." Nikki said, her gaze flickering at Duncan before it locked on Rayshad. "Give her a hug."

An awkward smile graced his lips as he got out of his seat.

"Your mom has told me a lot about you," Gina said, wiping her mouth with the back of an unsteady hand.

"Too bad I can't say the same," he said under his breath, with a scathing look in Nikki's direction. "Wow, Grandma," he said behind a smile that didn't quite reach his eyes. "It's really nice to meet you."

"Yeah, baby. We've got a lot to catch up on."

"Since you're up," Nikki suggested, "why don't you fix Carissa's plate?"

Carissa looked Nikki over and smiled. "Thank you so much for welcoming me into your home. It's very beautiful, by the way."

Nikki was charmed by her politeness. "Oh…sweetie, thank you. You are welcomed here any time."

Rayshad blushed when Nikki winked at him.

"What's this?" Gina asked, poking at the green stalks on her plate.

"That's asparagus, Ma."

"A-spare-a-*what?* I'm not eating it!" She shook her head and tossed the offending green vegetable onto her plate.

Nikki looked around the table, trying not to show how embarrassed she was by the outburst. "Well, don't, Ma. Duncan, give her salad instead."

"Nah, nah. Don't go through any trouble for me. Funny, though, when you get money, you eat some of the weirdest things."

"What's so weird about asparagus?"

"Isn't this the stuff pandas eat?"

"That's bamboo, Grandma," Rayshad said, trying to hold in his laughter. Carissa wasn't so lucky and nearly choked on a mouthful of turkey. He gently patted her back until she regained her composure. Duncan could only shake his head, and Nikki wondered what was going through his mind. He remained strangely silent for most of the dinner.

"Whatever. All I need is some chitlins, greens, maybe some butter beans, and some Jiffy cornbread, and I'm fine."

Is that what they fed you in jail? is what Nikki wanted to say, but instead, she replied, "Well, there's greens on your plate. I'm glad I cooked *something* you like."

She focused on Rayshad who was pushing his greens around the plate, disturbed that there was pork mingled in them. "We almost thought that you were skipping out on us."

"Carissa stays about twenty minutes away," Rayshad replied.

"Oh, okay." She smiled at Carissa. "So, tell me a little about yourself."

Carissa placed the fork onto her plate and looked over at Nikki. "I'm fifteen, but I'll be sixteen like Rayshad next month. And um, I sing in the choir with him at church."

"Oh, that's why you look so familiar. Do you go to school with him, too?"

Carissa lowered her gaze, finding a sudden interest in

her hands folded on her lap. "No. I go to a public school across town."

"Oh, okay." Nikki wondered why Carissa would be embarrassed by having to say those words. She encouraged her. "I get this 'smart' vibe from you. You've got good grades, don't you?"

Carissa looked up and smiled. "Yes."

Nikki returned an even brighter smile. "That's all that matters."

So far, she was impressed with her son's selection. Carissa was bright, beautiful, and church-going.

"So," Nikki said, weighing how to edge into dangerous territory, "are you guys boyfriend and girlfriend, or what?" She looked between Rayshad and Carissa, then glanced at Duncan whose fork paused midway in the path to his mouth, anxiously awaiting their response.

Carissa looked at Rayshad, her smile widening.

Rayshad grinned back at the anxious young woman and said, "Yes, Ma."

Duncan nodded as he resumed eating.

Nikki hid her excitement behind a sip of water.

"Why are you guys in this boy's business?" Gina passed her empty plate to Nikki. "Of course he's got a girlfriend! Now I'll take a little more of those yams over there. And what do you have for dessert? I've got a taste for some peach cobbler."

Nikki took the plate toward the kitchen and realized that it was going to be a long night.

Chapter Fifteen

Nikki woke up abruptly, gasping for air. Her chest heaved in an effort to catch a steadying breath. Darkness flooded her vision as images of a bullet blasting through a man's head echoed in her consciousness. When she saw blood sprinkled all over her body, Nikki yelped and aggressively tried to wipe it off of her. As her mind slowly snapped back to reality, she realized the moisture was only sweat.

She reached out to the other side of the bed to lie on Duncan, but found it empty.

Standing to her feet, she shot a look at the bathroom door, which was closed. *Duncan must have made a late-night trek to the throne*, she thought as she grabbed her silk robe and made her way downstairs to the kitchen.

Filling a black tea kettle with filtered water, Nikki glanced outside of the window. She had never been up this early and was still exhausted from hosting Thanksgiving dinner, but there was no point in making an attempt to finish out the rest of her slumber. Especially if nightmares were the only thing she could look forward to.

After setting the kettle on top of the stove, she walked to the other side of the room and leaned against the patio door.

It was still dark outside, but she could see how pitiful her vegetable garden looked. Since her mother's return, she hadn't set foot outside to do any of the things she loved. Tending to her garden had always been therapeutic, but nothing had worked since that day. She had thought about calling a gardener, but never seemed to get around to it. Maybe she'd get dirty today.

Water rumbled in the pot behind her.

Inviting Gina over for Thanksgiving had done nothing to settle Nikki's nightmares. In fact, they had gotten worse. Her mother's presence reminded her of things she tried her best to forget. The streets. Latrice. That fateful night.

The kettle let out a shrill, piercing sound. Nikki rushed to the stove and pulled it from the flame. She poured hot water over the tea bag before squeezing a little lemon into the cup.

The sound of quiet footsteps behind her caused her to tense up. She turned, wondering who was coming up the hallway.

Rayshad dragged into the kitchen with only pajama pants covering his bottom half. He rubbed eyes with a balled fist.

A short smile came to Nikki's lips. No matter what Rayshad thought, he was still a baby to her.

"You up?" she said as if it weren't obvious.

"Yeah," he replied with a wide yawn. "I thought you were screaming or something."

"And you came walking instead of running to see about me?" she asked in jest.

He smiled.

Nikki looked down at her cup, pressing the tea bag against the spoon while wrapping the string tightly.

"I want some," he said, walking up to his mother. "Why are you up so early?"

"Couldn't sleep." Nikki reached in the cabinet for another cup. "Had a bad dream."

"About what?"

Nikki tried to find the right words as she poured his tea and Rayshad followed her to the breakfast table. "You know, there are a lot of things about my childhood you don't know about."

"I know." Rayshad took a small sip, grimaced and reached for the sugar bowl and poured some in. "All this time I knew nothing about my grandmother."

"And I'm sorry about that."

There was a long moment of silence between the two of them. Occasional sips and setting the cups back on the saucers broke the stillness in the room.

"Ma," he said softly, cutting through the silence, "I think I'm old enough to know."

Nikki looked another direction.

"Why haven't you seen her all of these years?" He paused. "Or have you?"

Nikki closed her eyes for a moment before opening

them again and finding her son's gaze locked on her face.

Rayshad's chest rose and fell as though trying to keep his emotions in check. "You don't just spring that on someone, Ma. Do you know how embarrassed I was?" He pursed his lips. "When I took Carissa home, she asked me all kinds of questions that I couldn't answer. You didn't even say that she was coming for dinner."

"I didn't believe she would actually show up."

Rayshad crossed his arms.

"I…there are several things about my past that I haven't told you or anyone else about. They hurt too much to talk about."

"Like what?"

She exhaled, then took a small sip of tea. "I guess you're old enough to know."

Rayshad reached across the table and grabbed his mother's hand. She tightened the grip, took a deep breath, and looked into her son's eyes. All of his life, she'd kept a silver spoon in his mouth. He wouldn't know what a struggle was, even if it bit him. Would he understand the horrible things she'd gone through?

"I grew up a lot different from you." She looked down at their joined hands. "I know I told you I didn't have a mother, but the way things were, you might as well say that my mother didn't exist. She was never there for me or my little sister."

Rayshad tensed up. "You had a sister?"

Nikki nodded and felt guilty that she had not told her

son these things. "Latrice. We were both little girls when my father ended up leaving us for some other woman. At least, that's what my mother told me. My mother went crazy after he left, got hooked on drugs, and ran the streets. My mother hardly ever came home."

Rayshad sat up. "What was she doing in the streets? Like prostituting?"

"I'm not sure because I wasn't out there with her," she responded. "I learned how to take care of myself and my younger sister."

He stopped blowing on the steaming tea. "How? You were only a kid."

"Back then, we had neighbors with a lot of kids who cooked large meals and didn't mind if Latrice and I stayed over for dinner. Or we'd go to the store and take what we could without anyone knowing."

Rayshad's eyes grew to the size of egg yolks. "You mean, steal?"

She shrugged. "We did what we had to do."

"So what kind of drugs did Grandma do?"

Nikki squinted, then closed her eyes altogether. She vaguely remembered walking into her mother's cluttered room. Dirty clothes, shoes, hair weave, and empty bottles of beer had covered a raggedy, brown carpet. On the nightstand, a roach had crawled over a glass tube and a small bag of some white substance that sat next to a dusty lamp, needle, and crusty spoon. The bug had made an attempt to catch up to its friends on the other side of the nightstand.

Nikki blinked away that image but another one resurfaced immediately.

Rushing in the house from school, Nikki had run to the bathroom but had stood back when she had noticed the door cracked with the light on. She had leaned to the side and had noticed someone's reflection in the bathroom mirror. Gina was sitting on the toilet, her hair wild, with something hanging from her mouth.

Nikki had moved to get a better view.

Flicking a tall-flamed lighter, Gina had gripped a glass tube with her lips and had held it over the fire. Sucking it feverishly, a small amount of smoke had come from the pipe and had released a familiar odor Nikki had smelled plenty of times before—a smell she would never forget.

Watching her mother pull that poison into her body made Nikki wish she would have stayed away like she had all those other times.

"She did all kinds of stuff," Nikki said quietly. "I really couldn't tell you."

"So you….what? Why didn't you call the police or something?"

"She was my mother; even I knew that she was sick. All I knew was that I had to take care of Latrice. I never stopped going to school, because I looked forward to lunch. But, things caught up to me, because I eventually got arrested for shoplifting."

Rayshad gasped. "Arrested?"

"For trying to steal some canned goods and a pound of ground beef. They let me go after they found out why I did it, but that didn't make it right, though," she added sensibly. "They actually gave me a job. I never stole anything from them or anyone else again."

Rayshad smiled.

"But my mother did clean herself up one time. She came home after being gone for several months and was sober." Nikki smiled at that memory. "Her hair was freshly braided and she had on makeup—which was something I never saw her wear. And she smelled sweet like vanilla. I also remember the gold jewelry she wore. Now, *that's* how I knew she was clean and sober. Otherwise, she would have sold it all."

"Her addiction was *that* bad?"

"Bad enough for her to abandon her daughters!"

He leaned his head to the side and reasoned. "True."

"Latrice and I were really proud of her." Her smile slowly disappeared as the next set of events clicked into her memory. "But it was not long after that until something terrible happened."

Rayshad leaned in with wide eyes. "What?"

"She ended up moving Robert in with us. They used to argue all of the time, but nothing physical. But then one day I came home from work, and I could hear yelling inside of the house."

"Who was it? Grandma?"

Nikki nodded. "I ran into the house and found Latrice

standing in the dark hallway crying in front of the bedroom where all the commotion was coming from. She ran to me and started crying so hard she couldn't get a single word out. I had her stay back as I went into the bedroom."

Rayshad anxiously fiddled his fingers.

"My mom had a gun pointed a few inches away from Robert's head."

"Oh my God!"

"'Ma, what are you doing?'" Nikki whispered, even though there was only Rayshad to hear her. "My mom tried to tell me to stay out of it and get out of the room. Robert trembled and begged for her to put the gun down."

"Did she?"

"She shot him in the head."

Rayshad shook his head and pushed the cup off to the side.

"Blood and brains went everywhere. Even on me, but mostly on my mom. She fell to the ground crying over what she had done, but it was too late."

Nikki could still remember the coppery taste of blood as she had backed away from the scene. But not before seeing Robert's body fall back into the closet, leaking a huge puddle of dark red blood. The moment Nikki had bumped into Latrice who blocked the door, the little girl let out a blood-curdling scream.

The sound had spurred Nikki to action. "Come on, Latrice!" she had yelled and ran as far as her raggedy tennis shoes could carry her. The wind had slapped her in the face and had whispered in her ears. Her throat had burned from exhaustion and she had wanted to stop.

Boom!

That shot had played out again. She had closed her eyes and picked up the pace, running past the corner store, her high school, and the library. No destination in mind, simply away…

Pain had shot through her ankle but she had pressed on. She had bit her lip, trying to focus on nothing but her feet carrying her to a safe place. *Keep going*, she had told herself treading up the concrete before her. *Don't stop. Follow the yellow line.*

Their lives were so much more peaceful before Gina came back. It always took some time to adjust, but Nikki had created a routine for them to go by. One that worked for the two girls.

Headlights had approached, the car swerving out of the way just before hitting Nikki. She didn't look back when they had blasted their horn. *Run.*

There were sidewalks, but she didn't care. All that mattered was that she got away.

But Latrice.

Every time Gina had come back into their lives something had happened. Nikki should have run a long time, ago. If it wasn't for Latrice…

Nikki had looked back. But only once. She had wanted to see if Latrice had followed her somehow. She hoped her little sister had kept up, but wasn't sure. Nikki had kept running until there was nowhere left to run.

Tears had blurred her vision. She had ventured a look to her left and to her right and had seen that she was the only one there. Her little sister was nowhere in sight.

That was unfortunate because Nikki wasn't going back. Not even for Latrice.

❧ ❧ ❧

Nikki reached for a napkin at the center of the table and wiped her tears, focusing on the stretch of light breaking across the horizon. The coffeemaker clicked on and started growling. She rose from her seat and glided to the other side of the kitchen.

"Where did you go?"

Nikki opened the refrigerator and pulled out eggs, bacon, cheese, and butter. "I really didn't know where to go at first. But, I found a pay phone, called Duncan, and he came and got me. I stayed with him and his parents for the rest of the summer until my first year of college started."

"*You* went to college?"

Nikki grimaced, realizing that she hadn't told her son some of the good things that had happened in her life, either.

"For a couple years, back in the late eighties. That's where I met your father."

"Oh."

"Yeah. He was a junior when I was a freshman. I got pregnant around the time he graduated. Then we moved to Altadena." She pulled a coffee mug from the cabinet for Duncan. "Do you remember living there? You had to be about five years old before we moved to Bel Air."

Rayshad nodded. "Vaguely." He crossed his arms. "So what happened to Latrice?" he asked with a frown.

Nikki froze, the refrigerator door halfway to closing. "Ma?"

She inched over to the island counter and faced her son. "When I first moved on campus, I found out that Latrice was staying in a foster home. Of course, I couldn't get custody of her, so…I tried to get her to run away."

Rayshad perked up. "Did she?"

"I wanted her to. She told me all about the abuse she endured. She'd been…molested, had all these scars on her body. None of the social workers she told did anything to help her. I couldn't bear leaving her there."

"So did she run away?"

Nikki's mind flashed back to the last time she saw Latrice. Her foster parents had allowed Nikki to pick her up and so they could go to the movies and see *Purple Rain*.

"I don't want to take you back," Nikki had said while driving Latrice back home.

Latrice had bit her bottom lip and looked up into Nikki's eyes, hers filled with tears.

"We don't have to go back, Latrice. I can take you and we can move away somewhere."

"Where?" Latrice had asked. "Won't we get in trouble?"

Nikki couldn't tell her no, because kidnapping was a crime. "Nobody would know."

Latrice had shaken her head. "I don't want you to get in trouble, Nikki. What if you go to jail, too, like Ma? Then I won't have you. I won't have Ma. I won't have anybody."

Nikki's thoughts floated back to the present. Rayshad was still sitting at the table, anxiously awaiting her reply. "She didn't want to," she responded.

"Why?"

Nikki shrugged her shoulders. "Fear, I guess. But whatever it was, I know that she went through so much pain that she couldn't…" Nikki tried to speak around the lump in her throat. "She…she…couldn't take it anymore…"

Rayshad's mouth dropped open. "She killed herself?"

Nikki closed her eyes and took a deep breath.

"How?" Rayshad asked in a breathy whisper.

"I don't want to talk about it anymore." Nikki turned her attention to preparing breakfast. "Don't you need to get ready for school?"

Chapter Sixteen

Curled up on an Italian silk couch, Nikki sipped a steamy cup of green tea with one hand and held an open book with the other. Soft jazz played in the background of the dimly lit room with aromatherapy candles providing a relaxing mood. Duncan's smile flashed through her mind as she wondered if he had made it to his destination safely. He had promised that this trip to Sacramento would only be a couple of days. When he returned, she planned to surprise him with something, but had yet to decide what. She returned her attention to the words on the page and soon became lost in the story.

Twenty minutes later, headlights beamed through the window behind her. Rayshad hopped out of his Mustang and Carissa's head popped up from the other side. Nikki smiled. They had been dating for a couple of months and seemed closer than ever.

As the front door opened, Nikki marked her place in the book.

"Hey, Ma."

A smile stretched across her face. "Hey, you guys."

"Hi, Ms. Nik."

"Hey. Don't you look nice?" Nikki took to the young lady's jean skirt and matching jacket, accessorized with the diamond earrings and Gucci purse they had given her for her birthday and Christmas. Carissa was the only person Nikki knew whose birthday landed on Christmas Eve, which reminded her of Latrice, who had been born on New Year's Eve.

"Thank you," Carissa replied, smiling.

"I'll be right back," Rayshad said, jogging upstairs. "I left something."

"I was wondering why you came back so soon."

Carissa turned her attention to Nikki, whose nose was in the book. "What's that you're reading?" she asked, stepping forward to take in the title. "Oh, *The Things I Could Tell You*. That's one of my favorite books. I even wrote a book report on it for English class."

Nikki flipped the book closed, observing the solemn expression of the young man on the cover, which had been reflected in the eyes of her son at one time. "Really? It's pretty good, so far."

"What other books do you read?" Nikki placed the paperback in her lap. Besides cooking, reading novels was one of Nikki's favorite forms of entertainment. The fact that Carissa read for leisure said a lot about her.

Carissa named a few that Nikki had read herself. Her tastes varied from Terry McMillan to Mary Monroe.

"Have you read *Every Woman Needs a Wife* by Naleighna Kai?" she asked, taking a seat across from Nikki.

Nikki leaned forward. "I did and enjoyed it." She thought that particular book was a bit racy for the young lady, but the things she had been exposed to by the time she'd reached Carissa's age were far worse than any book.

"You know he's Naleighna's son," Carissa added, pointing to the novel in Nikki's lap.

Nikki looked down at the book. "Who? J. L. Woodson? Really?"

Carissa nodded. "Yep. I found out when I did my research on him."

Nikki tilted her head. "No wonder he's so talented at such a young age."

"He wrote that book when he was fifteen or something like that." Carissa shrugged. "You read a lot?"

"Yeah. I always buy a few books at a time and get way ahead of myself."

Carissa laughed.

"I'm catching up, though." She shrugged. "Maybe you can come book shopping with me one day. We'll make a girl's day out of it."

Carissa smiled brightly. "That would be so cool, Ms. Nik."

Nikki beamed. She liked when Carissa called her "Ms. Nik," which was so much more youthful sounding than Mrs. Johnson. "Great. Whenever's good for you is good for me."

Carissa's gaze shifted to the staircase.

Rayshad trotted downstairs with a brown suede jacket in his hand. He put his arm around Carissa's shoulder and led her to the door. "All right, Mom."

"All right, now. You two have fun. Be safe."

"Bye, Ms. Nik."

Nikki smiled. "Bye."

As the door closed behind them, Nikki wondered more about this girl that her son was falling in love with. If the two of them weren't on the phone for hours at a time, they were up under one another. Every morning, Rayshad would skip out on breakfast to pick Carissa up. In the afternoon, he escorted her from cheerleading practice so they could go to choir rehearsal together. He'd even traded in time shopping with his mother to go with Carissa instead.

But shopping was Rayshad's favorite thing to do, anyway. That's why Nikki wasn't surprised that they were currently headed to the mall.

Nikki turned over the novel in her hand, looking at the bold red letters of the author's name. "His mom *must* be proud." And that thought brought her son to mind. All she wanted was for him to go out into the world and make something of himself. Make her proud.

❧ ❧ ❧

Two weeks later, Nikki pulled her Corvette onto a broken asphalt driveway. Rocks crackled beneath her tires. Tall, thick grass sprung up between the cracks. Shielding her face from the sun with her hand, she took a good look at the dirty white house before her. Several shingles from the roof were missing—one on the ground next to an upside-down tricycle. A window appeared to be broken with a piece of cardboard and duct tape securing the hole. Two other windows had towels as drapes and the screen door no longer had a screen.

Was this where Carissa stayed?

She couldn't find the address from the street since the overgrown foliage covered it from view. Moving forward she finally made out the number posted on a raggedy column with chipped paint. Two of the numbers were upside down.

Nikki pulled herself out of the car and tiptoed carefully through the broken concrete. The front yard was made mostly of dirt with only two small patches of grass. Trash and toys were scattered about. Before Nikki could make it to the porch, the front door flung open and Carissa sprinted out.

"Come on, Ms. Nik." She walked so fast she almost tripped in her knee-high boots.

Nikki noticed Carissa's new hairstyle. Flat-twists in the front, waves on the side, waterfalls, and curls in the back, which made her look five years older than fifteen. She scoped out the new eye shadow and lip liner. Nikki remembered being Carissa's age, wanting to keep up with the latest trends but not having the means to do so. And from the looks of things, Carissa's family was pretty strapped for cash.

"Where's your mom? I wanted to meet her."

Carissa quickly ushered Nikki toward the driver's side. "Oh, she's at work."

Nikki narrowed her gaze at the young woman who scrambled over to the passenger side. "She said it was okay for you to come with me, didn't she?"

"Yep." Carissa was inside the car with her seatbelt strapped on in the same span of a single breath.

Nikki gave the house one last look before taking her place at the wheel. She put her seatbelt on and started the engine. Only when she pulled off did Carissa seem to breathe.

"I'm sorry that you had to come on this side of town to get me," Carissa said in a low voice.

"Oh no, sweetie. Don't apologize." Nikki hated that Carissa felt embarrassed about where she lived. It wasn't her fault, and she was pretty sure that if her mother had the choice, they wouldn't be staying there, either. "You know," she said, driving past several homes with lawns that needed to be cut. "I used to live not too far from here, myself."

Carissa's light-brown eyes widened and she tilted her head in disbelief. "No way!"

Nikki nodded, laughing. "I stayed a few blocks from here when I was your age."

"Seriously?"

"Yeah."

"I'm trippin' now, Ms. Nik," she said, with a slight giggle. "I didn't know you stayed in the 'hood. A true rags-to-riches story, huh?"

Nikki had never thought about it that way.

Carissa leaned forward to change the radio station until she came upon Beyoncé's "Irreplaceable." She bobbed her head and sang the lyrics as if she'd written the song herself.

They pulled into a parking lot a few minutes later.

Carissa looked around, puzzled. "Where are we exactly?" Several shops surrounded them, but there was not a bookstore in sight.

Nikki stepped out of the car. "I'm making a quick stop to get our nails done."

Carissa's eyes widened as she stood up out of the Corvette. "Really?"

"Of course, honey." Nikki guided them to the sidewalk before the outlet of stores. "What did you think a girl's day out was? We're about to get manis, pedis, and our eyebrows arched, too."

Carissa squealed like a five-year-old.

Nikki held the salon door open for her young guest. "After you."

As Carissa walked past her, Nikki's cell phone rang. She did not recognize the number, but answered it anyhow. "Hello?"

"Is this Nikki Johnson?" an unknown voice snapped, causing Nikki to bristle.

"Who is *this?*"

"This is Carissa's momma, Margaret Hudson."

Nikki stopped walking and shot a look at Carissa who had already made it to the front desk. "Oh…" It was about time she finally heard from her. She asked Carissa several times to have her mother call, but Margaret never did. But now that she had, why was she so angry?

"Is this Nikki?"

Nikki took a deep breath before she gave Margaret the kind of attitude she was shelling out. "This is. Is there a problem?"

"Ha! *Problem* isn't even the word, *Nikki!*"

Had she done something wrong?

"Look," Margaret continued, "I'm a hardworking woman. My feet hit the floor every morning for work—rain, sleet, snow, or shine. If I'm sick, I go. If my babies're sick, I *still* have to go. Half the time I'm working overtime. I do what I can to make sure my five kids don't need for anything. They may *want* some things that I can't provide, but that's a part of life."

Nikki smiled at Carissa when she turned around wondering why Nikki had not met her at the front desk yet. She held her finger up, asking her to hold on and stepped back outside for privacy.

"I'ma tell you what I don't need, though," Margaret continued. "I don't need you givin' handouts to my daughter like she's some goddamn charity case! Do you hear me?"

Nikki pulled the phone away from her ear and the woman's voice still came in loud and clear. But since she finally shut up, Nikki thought she could get a word in. "It's not even like that, Ms. Hudson. I—"

"I don't need nobody feelin' sorry for me, havin' sympathy for me and mine, tryna help me out like *I'm* not doing my job. If I needed help, I'd be the *first* one in line for a welfare check. I don't need you, the government, or nobody else playin' Momma for me—*alright?*"

Nikki took a deep breath and reminded herself to be the adult. "I understand, Ms. Hudson. With all the time my son spends with Carissa, she's like a daughter to me. She's so sweet, and my son loves her dearly—"

"*Son?* I would tell you how I really felt about that, but I'm not even gonna go there."

Nikki's head snapped up. "Don't hold back now."

"Look, Carissa *has* a boyfriend, okay? And it sure ain't that sissified son of yours!"

"That's it!" Nikki stomped. "I tried to keep my cool, but trust that I was doing *you* no favors being hospitable to your daughter, *Margaret*. And for you to call my phone with all this nonsense—it's beyond me."

When Nikki stopped talking, she realized that Margaret was still going off and probably didn't even hear her. "Talkin' 'bout Carissa's like a daughter to you! Who in the hell died and made you foster mama? Carissa has only one mama and you ain't it, bitch! Worry about your son gettin' fucked up the ass!"

Nikki disconnected the phone and gritted her teeth to keep from screaming. "What just happened?" she whispered to herself. When she turned around and looked through the glass door, Carissa was making her way outside. She contemplated whether or not she should take her back home right away, but didn't want to disappoint her.

"Everything okay?" Carissa asked, opening the door.

Nikki stepped inside and smiled, trying to hide her anger. "Everything's good," she lied. But she would tell her the truth on the way home.

❧ ❧ ❧

"Ms. Nik, I want to thank you for all that you do," Carissa said, looking at all of the shopping bags in the backseat. "I really appreciate it. Really, I do."

Nikki smiled as she segued the Corvette onto the freeway. "No problem, baby."

"I've gone through so much," the young woman said. "And you and Rayshad are the first people to really show me so much love."

When Nikki heard Carissa's voice tremor, she reached over and grabbed her hand. "Oh, sweetie." She wiped a tear from Carissa's cheek and had to look twice when she pictured Latrice. They favored one another even though Carissa was a few years older than her sister was when she last saw her. They even seemed to laugh the same way.

"More than anything I appreciate you inviting me to dinner all the time," Carissa said, trying to smile. "Your cooking sure tastes better than those Ramen noodles every day…" Then, as though she realized how that statement had sounded, she quickly added, "It's not really my mother's fault…I guess. She does all she can do. She works so hard to pay the bills that sometimes she's not around to cook. And when she is, she's too tired."

Nikki's brow furrowed at the thought of Carissa's mother. Was this a good time to tell her about the phone conversation she'd had with her earlier? Not with tears in Carissa's eyes, it wasn't. "You can come eat dinner with us any time, honey," Nikki replied, not caring how resentful Margaret was. "You don't have to wait for me to invite you, either. And when I teach you how to cook, I'll also show you how to use simple things to make meals for your family. Do you take vitamins?"

Carissa shook her head.

"Well, I'm about to stop and pick some up, okay?"

"Thank you, Ms. Nik." Carissa tried to smile, but failed. Her tight eyes filled with a grief that made Nikki's heart catch. "I've never had someone care so much. Not even my mom."

Nikki knew from her own experience that mothers were not always nurturing, but she didn't know how to respond to Carissa's admission, so she said nothing but held her hand tight.

"A couple of years ago"—she paused, fighting back the tears—"this man…he raped me."

Nikki's heart dropped into her stomach. "Oh my God."

"My mother didn't believe me when I told her, either." Her voice broke as tears spilled over her red face.

"How could—" Nikki felt her own tears forming, but blinked them away. "Your mother didn't *believe* you? Oh…honey! I'm sorry that you went through that. I couldn't imagine. I would've hunted that man down!"

Carissa wiped her tears and looked outside of the window.

Nikki didn't know whether what she had said made things better or worse. "I'm really sorry, Carissa, really. I want you to remember that when you feel you have no one else in your corner, I don't care if it's your mother or your teacher or hell—even Rayshad, just know that you've got me."

Nikki had not gone through everything Carissa had, but she knew what it was like to need an adult other than her own mother. Duncan's mother had fulfilled that need for Nikki when she was in high school. Had it not been for her influence on Nikki's life, she wouldn't know where she would be today.

Nikki looked over at Carissa who had a new sparkle of hope in her eyes. "Thank you, Ms. Nik."

"No problem, baby," she said, driving past the exit to Carissa's home. "Before I take you home, let's go back to my house and show Rayshad all of the things we got you."

Carissa smiled. "Okay."

Nikki already knew that Rayshad wouldn't care about

their girls' day out, but that was the only excuse she could think of to get out of dropping Carissa off. The last thing she wanted to do was deal with Margaret face-to-face, so Rayshad would be the one taking her home. She also wanted Carissa and Rayshad to see one another in case it would be the last time. Because at this point, there was no telling if her conversation with Margaret would lead to the end of their relationship.

Chapter Seventeen

Nikki switched her phone from one ear to the other, laughing at her mother. "I knew the day would come when you'd get frustrated with that thing."

"This darn phone," Gina muttered. "I don't understand why it hangs up on people."

When Nikki had bought Gina the phone for Christmas, she'd wondered how quickly her mother would grasp the new technology. She was still having trouble with how unreliable it was at times.

"But anyway, baby, how are you?"

"I'm okay," Nikki replied, stirring a sprinkling of seasoning into a pot of simmering sauce. "How was your weekend?"

"It was okay. Went to church and helped out with the youth."

Nikki smiled, glad that her mother was going to church. Something she hardly ever did but needed to. "That's good, Ma."

"How was your weekend?" Gina asked.

"It was okay." Nikki set the spoon to the side. "Took Carissa shopping and you wouldn't believe what happened."

"What?"

Nikki walked slowly toward the window and looked over her garden that had wilted since the beginning of winter. "Carissa's mother went off on me."

"For what?"

"I don't know."

"Had to be something," Gina countered.

Nikki shrugged. "Because I've done a couple of things for her, I guess."

"Like what?"

"Nothing really. Rayshad and I have gotten her a couple of things, but nothing that her mother should be upset about. Now, she's accusing me of making a charity case out of her and Carissa."

"Why would you be taking her shopping, anyway?"

"Because, I wanted to get to know her a little better—this girl who's dating my son." Nikki couldn't believe that she was now defending herself to her mother. "Besides, she's a nice girl, who does very well in school. She deserves to be rewarded for her accomplishments."

"Mmm."

"Anyway, I was calling you, because I'm getting dinner together. Duncan should be home any minute, and I wanted to invite you over."

"Yeah? Uh…well…"

"What's wrong, Ma?" Nikki tapped the spoon against the side of the pot a few times and set it to the side. Leaning her hip against the counter, she crossed her arms. Her mother still hadn't responded to her question.

"I think I'll…pass."

"Why?" Nikki demanded, eyeing the clock. Duncan should be walking through the door from his trip any minute.

"I…I don't feel comfortable in that big old house."

"Comfortable in my house? You feel comfortable in that dangerous neighborhood you stay in, but not in *my* house?"

"This apartment suits me fine; thank you very much."

"I'm sure it does, Ma," Nikki said, picturing the roach-infested apartment complex her mother called home.

"And I can't quite put my finger on it, but I don't like that Duncan fellow."

"What? How could you *not* like Duncan? What has he done to you?"

"He's done nothing to me. It's something about him. I got a bad vibe."

"Well, I don't know why you would think ill of him. He's a great husband. A good role model for Rayshad, always encouraging and supporting him in everything he does."

Gina gave a small, bitter laugh.

"Better than I could say for his own father."

"Yeah. Well. How is my grandson, by the way?"

"He's fine."

"Mmm."

Nikki's eyes lowered to slits. "Let me ask you something." She placed her hand on her hip. "Why is it I get this feeling that you're criticizing everything I tell you—everything about me? Whether it's where I live, who I marry, give birth to, hang out with…?"

"I'm not judging you, Nikki."

"Yes you are. And on top of that, you won't even accept my invitation to come over for dinner."

Gina said nothing.

"Then you act like nothing ever happened." Nikki held the phone for what seemed like eternity before her mother replied.

Still silence.

Nikki sighed. "Well…are you going to say anything?"

Gina took a deep breath. "I know I haven't been the best mother. And I remember there was a time that I loved those drugs more than I loved myself—more than I loved my own daughters. But when I cleaned myself up in '85, I made a vow to make all of that up to you. And Latrice."

Tears dropped from Nikki's eyes.

"Robert was a man I met in rehab. We were both committed to one another and supported each other's road to recovery. But one day, I walked in on him doing something I never would have expected."

"What? Did he relapse?"

"He was touching your little sister."

Nikki's chest tightened and she grew numb all over.

"I snapped," Gina continued. "No words. Nothing. I went to my room, grabbed my pistol, and…and…I didn't feel. I just…did."

Flashbacks of her younger sister standing in the hallway crying just before she'd witnessed her mother's crime popped into her mind. Latrice's moods had transformed after Robert had appeared and Nikki always wondered why.

"Are you serious, Ma? Oh my God."

Gina sniffed.

"You should have never gone to jail, Mom. I can't believe—" Tears dripped from Nikki's eyes.

"Yeah, well. I didn't think so, either. The justice system failed me. And when you ran away, I knew I failed you, too."

Guilt struck Nikki like a lightning bolt. "I'm sorry, Mom."

"Yeah, well…" Gina sighed. "That's all in the past, now. Don't cry. I'm glad that I have a chance to be with my daughter, again."

Nikki heard the front door close. "I'm glad that you're back, too, Ma."

"Well, get back to cooking," Gina replied. "I'm about to do a little cooking of my own."

"All right, Ma. But hey!" Nikki said before Gina hung up.

"Yeah?"

Nikki took a deep breath. "I love you." She could not remember the last time they expressed their love for one another.

"Love you, too."

Duncan walked in the room as Nikki hung up the phone.

"Hey, baby! I missed you." Duncan kissed Nikki and glanced at the pots on the stove. "Who was that? Your mom?"

Nikki opened a cabinet and pulled a few plates out. "Yeah. How did you know?"

"Your mother *better* be the only person you're saying 'I love you' to."

Nikki laughed. "Yeah. I don't know what's up with her."

"Why do you say that?"

She hesitated before telling him. "She doesn't like you."

"Me? What did I do?"

Nikki shrugged. "She gets this *feeling* about you. But then, I'm also thinking it might not even be you. I believe she thinks I've forgotten where I come from, you know?"

"Well, we *know* that you haven't forgotten that," he replied. "And if she feels that way, so what? My family felt the same way when I first started making money. And after a few handouts, they got over it."

She tried to force a laugh.

"But her not liking me—that's another story."

✿ ✿ ✿

Nikki smiled when Duncan walked into the dining room with wide eyes, gazing at dinner spread from one end of the table to the next.

"Wow," Duncan said, taking a seat. "You never cease to amaze me. What's the occasion?"

"Nothing special," she replied, shrugging. She shot a look at Rayshad who was sitting across the table texting on his cell phone, his thumbs flying wildly about. Guilt filled her chest as she imagined what trouble she might have caused after the altercation with his girlfriend's mother. He had not said anything about it, but she wondered what he knew.

After blessing the food, Nikki grabbed a dish, dumped a small portion of casserole on her plate, and passed it to Duncan. "So how was your trip?"

"Nothing special. Couldn't wait to get home. Met up with this guy. We talked about closing a deal later this month." Duncan had bags under his eyes. "Seven digits. It's commercial, though. You know I'm used to dealing with residential."

Nikki sipped a glass of water and set it down. "That's good." Big money was hardly any news. She was used to her husband dealing with multimillion-dollar properties.

Rayshad hadn't touched his plate, as his eyes were glued to his cell phone, but he still managed to keep up with their conversation. "I might need to think about this whole real estate thing," he said.

"What happened to becoming a model or a singer?" Nikki asked.

"He can still do that *and* invest on the side." Duncan was putting a serious dent into his food.

"For real?" Rayshad looked across the table at his step-father; his thumbs frozen above the miniature keyboard.

Duncan nodded. "Investing in real estate can be a part-time thing. For a person who already has money—and good credit—it's a pretty easy thing to do. You can build wealth in no time."

Rayshad nodded, placed his phone on the table and reached for a plate.

"Listen to Duncan," Nikki said. "Any man who can make it from zero to millions can give you some pretty good advice." She shot a look at Duncan who grinned at her compliment.

"Zero?" Rayshad gasped. "I thought that you *always* had money, man."

Duncan smiled as he chewed his food. "Not all rich people have always been rich, like not all homeless people have always been poor. It's all in the decisions you make in life." He stabbed a baked chicken breast. "You only have one life to live, so I suggest you follow your dreams while you're still young. Study hard. Stay in school. All of those things will benefit you in the long run."

"What college did you go to?"

Duncan looked up at Rayshad and then to Nikki who gave a small, almost unnoticeable, shake of her head.

"Well, I didn't exactly go to college."

"You didn't? And you're *still* a millionaire?"

Duncan laughed again. "Not *all* millionaires have a college education. I know some who stopped at the eighth grade."

"I'm educated more than that!" the high school junior exclaimed.

Nikki cleared her throat, trying to get Duncan's attention.

"True, but that doesn't mean you should stop what you're doing in hopes that you'll make it big one day." Duncan took a bite of broccoli. "Different things work for different people."

"So, I *should* go to college, even though *you* didn't?" Rayshad asked, a sly smile on his thin lips. Then he looked at his mother. "Even though my mother didn't?"

Nikki's fork hit the plate. "I went to college, remember? I just didn't finish." And it wasn't that she didn't want to go back to school, either. She tossed an angry glare in Duncan's direction, who skillfully avoided making eye contact and took a sudden interest in a third helping of her casserole. Any time she asked Duncan about going back to school or taking some online courses, he changed the subject or told her, "We'll see." He'd spent top-dollar on getting her breasts enlarged, but made a bunch of excuses when she mentioned school.

The doorbell rang.

Rayshad dropped his phone and hopped up. "I'll get it," he chimed, sprinting through the door separating the living and dining rooms.

Nikki sat up straight. "Wonder who that could be." They rarely had guests and her neighbors never stopped by.

"Maybe it's Carissa," Duncan replied, forking over a piece of salmon. "Haven't seen her in a while."

"Maybe, but who would've brought her? She doesn't have a car."

Suddenly, the sound of crying faintly loomed from another room. Who was that? Nikki wiped her lips and left the napkin next to her plate as she hurried toward the living room.

Peering from the dining room toward the front door, she found Carissa crying on Rayshad's arm, soaking the entire left side of his sweater. For once he didn't seem to care that his clothes were being soiled.

She walked slowly toward the couple and wondered what she should say. The last thing Nikki wanted to do was make things worse. She rubbed the young girl's arm as Rayshad avoided eye contact. When Carissa turned to see Nikki, she wailed and buried her head into Rayshad's chest.

"Carissa, I—" Nikki stopped herself before apologizing. Maybe Carissa wasn't crying because of the argument with Margaret. "What's wrong?"

"Ma…there's something we need to tell you." Rayshad held his girlfriend close as he looked out of the window.

Nikki straightened up slowly.

Duncan entered the room. "Hey. Is everything okay?"

Rayshad looked away. "You guys, Carissa is…she's pregnant."

Nikki froze. Carissa's weeping ebbed to near silence. Her vision slowly faded into darkness as Duncan caught her the moment her knees gave out.

"Oh my God!" Carissa shrieked, tearing away from Rayshad.

"Ma!"

Duncan carried her limp body like a baby and placed her on the sofa on the opposite side of Rayshad. "Nikki!" He tapped her face. "Nikki, baby!"

Nikki's eyes fluttered open to find Duncan's hand waving before her.

"Baby, are you okay?"

Nikki sat up, struggling to regain her composure. Rayshad's lip trembled. Carissa had covered her face with shaking hands.

"I'll be right back." Duncan jogged to the kitchen.

The word "pregnant" kept ringing through Nikki's mind. "Oh my God," she whispered, then scanned the worried faces of the two youngsters. "How do you know for sure?"

"We had sex, Ms. Nik," Carissa murmured through her hands.

Nikki pressed a hand to her temple. "No. What I mean…" Duncan tried to hand her a glass of water. She passed it back. "Wine. Please." She turned her attention back to the other two. "What I mean is—have you been to a doctor?"

Carissa shook her head. "I took a home pregnancy test, though."

"Well, those aren't always reliable," she replied, an ounce of hope filling her heart.

When Duncan returned, she downed the entire glass of wine in one pass as the telephone started ringing.

Rayshad answered. "Hello?" Seconds later, he removed the phone from his ear and held it out. "It's for you, Ma."

Nikki took the phone. "Hello?"

"She's all yours, now."

Nikki squinted her eyes until she made out Margaret Hudson's voice. "Excuse me?"

"You said she was the daughter you never had, so let her put you through hell like she's done me these past few years. Now that her fast ass has gone and got knocked up, I'm through with her. I told her and my three other girls that if they ever got pregnant, I was putting my hands up with them. Go live with the baby's daddy, for all I care."

"You can't be serious?"

"As a heart attack! But I packed up all her belongings. They're out here in the car."

Nikki moved to the other side of the room and looked out of the window. A small red Ford Focus with a faded hood was parked in the driveway.

"That little boyfriend of hers can come out and help her get it all."

Instead of cursing Margaret out and telling her how she really felt, Nikki disconnected the call.

"Who was that?" Duncan asked.

Nikki looked at Carissa who asked, "Was that my mom?"
She nodded.

"So, I guess she told you." Carissa's face turned even redder than it was before. She shot a quick look at both Nikki and Duncan, then looked down.

"She did," Nikki said glumly. She walked toward the stairs leading to the second level. "I guess I'll get a room ready for you. Rayshad, go help her with her bags. And don't say a single word to her mother."

Carissa glanced at Rayshad who had a worried look on his face.

"I'll take you to a doctor when you get home from school," she added, looking over her shoulder, hoping this was a false alarm.

Hopefully. But she had her doubts.

Chapter Eighteen

"Wake up!" Nikki yanked the purple comforter from over Carissa's face.

Carissa rolled over and buried her head into the pillow.

Nikki frowned, and shook the slumbering body more vigorously. "Wake up, girl! You know it's time for school."

Carissa's eyes cracked open and she rubbed her face. "I don't want to go to school."

"Too bad," Nikki replied. "Nothing's changed because you moved here. You still have to go to school *every* day."

Carissa groaned.

Nikki clapped her hands loudly. "Come on," she said, stepping over a pair of shoes in the middle of the floor. "Let's go!" She closed the door behind her, shaking her head. Why did she have to go through this every day? She couldn't think of the last time she had to wake Rayshad this way.

"Good morning, Ma," he said, breezing past her in the hallway, wearing a peach shirt. A trail of his cologne lingered behind him as he jogged downstairs.

"Hey, baby." She followed him into the kitchen from the staircase.

Sitting in front of his breakfast plate, Rayshad greeted Duncan who flicked a newspaper with one hand and sipped coffee with the other. He wore a sky blue dress shirt similar to Rayshad's. Nikki smiled at them for wearing the dress shirts she had bought for them a week ago on the same exact day.

"Have you been looking for a job?" she asked, carrying a couple of pans from the stove to the sink.

Rayshad scooped a spoonful of pineapple and didn't bother to answer.

She leveled a look at him. He knew she was talking to him.

"I'm too busy with school."

Nikki placed her hand on her hip. "You've been busy doing a *lot* of things, and that's why you're in the mess that you're in."

Duncan glanced up from his newspaper.

Rayshad exhaled loudly, pushed his chair back, and stood.

"Sit down," Nikki ordered.

He slung his book bag over his shoulder and walked out.

"Hey," Nikki called.

The door slammed shut behind him.

Duncan glanced at Nikki. When she glared at him, he looked away.

Nikki snatched a wet towel from the sink and scrubbed the counter furiously. With the baby's arrival in three months, Rayshad and Carissa needed to prepare themselves for this life-changing event. How could she get them to see that? Did they expect to be pacified? To have the responsibility of caring for their child passed on to someone else?

She turned to see Carissa trudge into the kitchen. The girl wasn't all that cute at first light. Her hair was all over her head, and she wore an old T-shirt and baggy sweat-pants.

"You okay?" Nikki asked.

"No," Carissa said with a sour look on her face. "I just threw up." She rubbed her rounded stomach.

"Well, that's morning sickness for you," Nikki replied casually, running water over the dirty dishes. The whole situation still left a bad taste in her mouth. She refused to be sympathetic to either one of them.

Nikki pulled a plate from the cupboard. "You want breakfast?"

"So I can throw up again?" Carissa said, with a frown. "I want to lay down."

"I won't let you be late for school." Nikki set the plate down and looked at Carissa who pursed her lips.

"I'm not eating that."

"Fine. Then go on and get dressed," Nikki instructed. "I'll be taking you to school today."

"Where's Rayshad?"

"He's already gone to school," Nikki snapped, tired of the girl's whiny voice. "He told me you were taking too long." She shot a look at Duncan.

Carissa folded her arms over her gray nightshirt and smacked her lips. "That's messed up."

"No, it's not! Your school is on the other side of town. *You're* late getting up. He didn't need to be late, too. Now, go on." She watched Carissa exit the room.

Duncan turned a page in the newspaper. "Why'd you tell her that?"

Nikki rolled her eyes and removed the plate from before him that he'd licked clean. "Tell her what?"

Looking up from the paper, he grinned. "You told her that Rayshad left because she was taking too long. You know you upset that boy."

"Whatever," Nikki snapped. "She needs to learn how to function like everyone else around here. That girl's been here for two weeks already and I've had to wake her up every single day. She's not about to sit up here and be lazy."

Duncan folded the newspaper and stood.

"You off to work?" she asked, loading the dishwasher with dishes.

"Yep." He downed the rest of his coffee, then gave his wife a kiss before he left.

As soon as she heard the door close, Nikki called out to Carissa. "Are you ready to go?" The house was so big, Nikki didn't know why she bothered calling out. She wiped her hands with the dishtowel and headed upstairs toward what was now considered Carissa's room.

Pushing the door open, Nikki found the young lady sprawled across the bed. Soft snores came from under the covers.

"Uh-uh," Nikki said, taking a good look around.

Since Carissa had moved in, the guest room had become the junkiest room in the house. Clothes were all over the place, books and papers were strewn about, and three sticky glasses sat on the nightstand. Nikki refused to be her maid. Rayshad kept his room immaculate, and she expected the same of Carissa.

She shook the body underneath the comforter. "Get up, Carissa! I'm not playing with you."

Carissa pulled herself up and groaned. "I really don't wanna go today, Ms. Nik. I'm so sick."

"But what about all the days you weren't sick and you still begged me to let you stay home? If you aren't sick, you're too tired."

"I can't go," she whined. "I'm tired of people staring at me and my belly."

Crossing her arms over her full breasts, Nikki huffed. "Whatever, Carissa. You *still* have to go."

Carissa looked up at Nikki giving her the best pitiful puppy-dog look she could manage.

"What are you going to do? Get a job?" Nikki asked.

"I want to do what you do."

Nikki's eyebrows rose. "And what do you think that is?"

The young lady shrugged. "I don't know, shop all day."

Nikki stepped back. *"Shop all day?"* Evidently Carissa hadn't paid attention to all of the things she did in a day. Slaving over the stove for hours. Cleaning each room of the mansion. And the type of shopping she did for the household was not all pleasure. "Honey, being a house-wife is *not* that easy."

"Well, you make it look easy."

Nikki didn't know whether to take that as a compliment or not. "I tell you what," she said, sitting down beside Carissa on the bed. "I'll let you take this day off."

Carissa sat up, giving her a wide smile.

"But you're not about to lay around here doing nothing at all." She placed her arm around Carissa's back. "Since you think being a housewife is so easy, I'm going to put you to the test. And by the end of the day, we'll see if this is something that you still want to do."

&a &a &a

Sweating and breathing hard, Nikki jogged through the front door and kept moving in place. She checked her pulse as she spotted Carissa lying on the couch watching television. Nikki knew that she wasn't finished with all of her chores. It was only nine o'clock in the morning.

"You're finished with everything *that* fast?" she asked.

Carissa looked away. "You *know* I'm not." She picked up the remote and changed the channel. "There's no way I could have finished cleaning one bathroom, let alone this whole house by now!"

Nikki stepped in front of the television and turned it off. "Yeah, well, it's all in a day's work."

Carissa exhaled hopelessly.

"Okay. Break time's over. Hurry up, so we can start making dinner."

"Dinner? *This* early?" Carissa looked at the clock on the wall. "It's not even lunchtime."

"Not now. In a couple of hours."

Carissa looked as if she still couldn't believe her.

"I cook all of my food from scratch, so it takes much longer than…Top Ramen. You'll see."

"And what about this?" Carissa asked, holding her broom up. "What are you going to do?"

"What do you mean?"

"I'm saying, you're not going to clean up anything?"

Nikki's chin went down. "I assigned those chores to *you*. Don't forget that you're taking my place for the day. See what a day in the life of Nikki Johnson is *all* about."

Carissa poked her lip out, but Nikki didn't care.

"I'm about to go run some errands—or what do you call it?" Nikki snapped her fingers. "Oh, yeah, shopping."

≈ ≈ ≈

"Carissa!" Nikki yelled, slicing the last of a garden tomato. That was her second time calling out to get the girl's attention. Nikki didn't care how angry Carissa was about her chores, but intentionally ignoring her was only going to make things worse.

Rayshad walked into the kitchen right before Nikki yelled for her again.

"Oh hey."

"Hey." He picked up an apple from the fruit bowl and took a bite.

"Where's Carissa?" she asked.

"She's 'sleep."

"Oh, really?" Nikki asked, placing her knife down.

She marched out of the kitchen, wiping her hands on her apron and headed to Carissa's room. When she opened the door, she found the young lady lying in bed, sleeping peacefully.

Nikki smiled at the tired girl as the sound of victory rang in her ears. Evidently Carissa figured out she was not suited to be a housewife. First thing tomorrow, she would be taking her butt back to school *and* looking for a job.

She went back to the kitchen and smiled at Rayshad who sat at the breakfast table, nibbling on cheese crackers and flipping through a magazine.

"She's still 'sleep?" he asked.

"Yes." Nikki picked up the knife and finished slicing the tomatoes.

He looked up from his notebook; his face filled with worry. "I hope she's okay."

"She's tired. Something all pregnant women go through."

"Oh."

Nikki noticed that the magazine Rayshad flipped through was an *Ebony*. "Are you two still a couple?"

Rayshad looked up. "Yeah, why?"

"You don't seem as close as before." Nikki searched her son's face.

"Things *have* changed, and I don't know why. I...I don't know. Then, she gets an attitude with me when I haven't even done anything."

Nikki giggled and returned to preparing the salad. "That's a part of being pregnant, Rayshad."

"Well, she doesn't have to make *me* suffer." He flipped through the pages of the magazine slowly.

"Trust me. She's suffering more than you are. All of these changes are happening not only to her body, but her hormones are affecting her attitude. Didn't you read the books I bought you?"

Rayshad shrugged. "Whatever. I stay as far away from her as possible. I'm tired of arguing."

"Yeah. I know how that is." Nikki thought back to her declining relationship with Chance and wondered how they were able to stay together for as long as they did. Arguing had become a part of their daily routine.

Nikki added the sliced tomatoes to a bowl of salad and grabbed an avocado. Rayshad's chair slid across the floor and soon footsteps approached the island.

"Ma, there's something I want to talk to you about."

"What?" She separated the large seed from the green substance.

"Ma…"

Nikki turned to see her son's puppy dog eyes filled with worry.

"I think she's lying," he said quietly. "I don't think that's my baby."

Nikki glared at Rayshad. "What?"

"Ma, I'm serious."

"What makes you think this, *now?* You had sex with the girl!"

"Yeah, but the dates don't match up."

Nikki crossed her arms across her chest. "How do you figure?"

Rayshad's shoulders went up and down. "I got a feeling, Ma."

"Feeling? That's it? You know you were with her, so be a man about it."

She resumed dicing the avocado, cutting even faster than before.

"Fine, but when she has the baby, I'm getting a DNA test." His tone was strong.

An eerie silence filled the room. "Have you told her that?"

"No."

She held up her hand. "Well, don't."

The doorbell rang.

She looked back at Rayshad. "Expecting company?"

He shook his head.

Nikki rinsed her hands and wiped them with her apron as she made way to the front door. Rayshad followed behind her into the living room, diving into the couch, magazine in hand.

She didn't bother scolding him for putting his feet up on the couch, because when she looked through the peephole, she found an unfamiliar lady standing outside with a baby on her hip.

Chapter Nineteen

Nikki couldn't breathe. Her nose was so stuffed up that all it could do was make a disgusting noise when she inhaled. Three days had passed since discovering Duncan's affair and love child, but she was still agonizing. Nikki hadn't felt this kind of pain since Trina had unveiled her secret affair with Chance. Now Duncan had betrayed her.

She wasn't comfortable in her hotel room, which had become her home for the past couple of days since an hour after meeting Marie. But she made do.

She shot a look at her luggage sitting in front of the bathroom door and saw herself packing again. Duncan had kept knocking on the bedroom door, begging for forgiveness. Her heart had pounded against her chest as she stuffed her bags with as much clothing as she could. When she'd finally opened the door, Duncan grabbed her softly. She'd looked into his eyes, and for the first time ever, saw tears. "Nikki, please." She'd tried to push him away, but like a sad puppy he followed her to the garage. He almost didn't move until she'd threatened to run him over. Thirty minutes later, Nikki had checked into the Beverly Hilton and made a trip to the bar.

Nikki stayed locked in her room, only opening the door for room service. Where had she gone wrong in life? She had already failed with her first marriage and now this one was on shaky ground. Even though divorce was not on her list of options, it was something that still floated across her mind each time she thought about how deceptive Duncan had been. And now Rayshad. Were all of these events haunting her because of what she had done in her youth? She was only nineteen when she'd betrayed Chance and conceived her son by another man. Karma couldn't be that brutal.

Wiping her puffy eyes, she realized she had cried so much that her face stung. When she had finally run out of tears, she pulled herself to the edge of the bed and grabbed her phone, which had been on silent since Duncan would not stop calling her that night.

"Nikki, pick up the phone," he cried on a voice mail message. *"We need to talk this through."*

DELETE.

"Can you please answer? Text me. Let me know where you are. Tell me you're okay."

Instead of listening to the rest of the many messages he'd left, she erased them as they came in.

If it weren't for Rayshad, she would not have thought twice about going back home. They spoke every morning before he went to school.

"Are you still mad with Duncan?" Rayshad asked.

Nikki blinked. "I don't want to talk about him, right now."

"When are you coming home? You know Carissa's going to have her baby any day now."

"I know. And I don't know when I'm coming home."

"You're not thinking about divorcing Duncan, are you?"

Nikki looked at the time on her phone. "Aren't you supposed to be on your way to school?"

"I am. But I miss you."

She closed her eyes. "I miss you, too."

"And your cooking."

Nikki smacked. "Tell the truth. *That's* what you really miss."

They laughed.

"I'll be home soon," she said. "I need some time to myself right now."

"Well, don't stay away too much longer."

She could hear the sadness in her son's voice. Flashbacks of times Gina had abandoned her and Latrice flowed into her mind. "I won't," she reassured. When they hung up, Nikki took a long, deep breath, and tilted her head back. She was going to have to face Duncan sooner or later.

≿ ≿ ≿

Pulling up into the driveway next to Rayshad's Mustang, Nikki eyed the clock as it struck 12:02 p.m. Why was he not in school? She pulled the brake, grabbed one of her bags, and stepped out of the car. As she unlocked the front door, she heard rap music faintly blasting from a room upstairs in the back. She dropped her bag and marched upstairs.

The music blaring from Rayshad's room got louder as she approached his door. Had he been skipping school for the past couple of days since she hadn't been home? He had some serious explaining to do.

"Rayshad!" She turned his doorknob, pushed the door open, and gasped. "Oh my—what the hell is going on in here?"

Rayshad jumped up and covered himself with the blanket. "Oh, shit!" He ran to the other side of the room to throw on some clothes.

Nikki stepped into the hallway and slammed the door behind her. She covered her chest with her hand and felt her heart beating so fast she thought it would leap out of her chest. She leaned against the wall and slid down to the hardwood floor, too shocked to scream or cry.

Rayshad's door flung open and he kneeled to her side. "Ma," he said, pulling her up.

Nikki stood up and stormed away, but Rayshad followed behind her. "I'm sorry you had to see that. I didn't know you were coming home, and—"

Nikki pulled away from her son's grasp and pointed a finger at him. "So, now it's *my* fault for coming home?"

"No," Rayshad said, hugging her in spite of her resistance. "Look, Mom. I'm sorry. I…I didn't know how to tell you the truth."

Nikki shrugged her shoulder away from Rayshad and looked him in the eyes. "And what *is* the truth, Rayshad? Be *real* with me, okay? I'm tired of all these goddamn surprises!"

"Okay, Ma! Okay!" Rayshad threw his arms up. "I'm gay! Okay?"

Images of what she had witnessed a few minutes ago flooded her mind. "Why didn't you tell me?" Nikki couldn't stop shaking her head. "You have a girlfriend and everything. How would Carissa feel about this? Does she know?"

"No," he replied quickly. "And don't tell her, either, Ma." Rayshad grabbed her hand and gave it a gentle squeeze. "Please."

Nikki looked at her only child and wondered if she would ever be able to erase the image of her son bending over in front of another man. The *last* thing she wanted to do was tell anybody.

"Where is Carissa?"

"I dropped her off at her mom's." He shoved his hands in his pockets nervously. "Margaret wanted to see her."

"After all this time? Really?"

Footsteps behind them caused her to turn and she hated what she saw. "Get out of my house!" she yelled, turning her head away from Rayshad's friend, Tony.

Rayshad walked toward his friend.

"No!" Nikki stood and pulled at his shoulder. "Where do you think you're going?"

"I'm going to drop him off, Ma."

Nikki watched her son guide the tall, dark young man out of the door with his hand on his back. Numbness covered her body as she tried best not to scold herself for being so naïve. When she heard his car drive away, she fell to her knees and cried.

Chapter Twenty

Nikki rapped her knuckles repeatedly against a door with chipped paint. When she saw an enormous roach crawl up the wall, she stepped back in terror. It had been over twenty years since she had seen one until she started visiting her mother. Gina's apartment was filled with them even though she kept her home spotless.

Nikki looked back when an old Chevy pulled up in a parking space behind her, booming loud music. Three spaces down, two men leaned against an old car smoking a joint. She quickly turned around and pounded on the door until she heard: "Who is it?"

"It's me, Ma."

Then she heard her mother unlocking the door from the other end. Gina still cracked the door first, before letting Nikki in.

"I didn't wake you, did I?" Nikki asked, forcing a smile. She stepped inside and tried to ignore the smell of the apartment. An old, stale odor that no matter how much her mother scrubbed the place down, never went away.

Gina shifted the pink satin bonnet on her head and yawned as she stepped into the adjoining kitchen. "I'm up," she said, smoothing her long nightgown. "Have a seat."

Nikki checked the couch for roaches before she sat down. The last time she'd visited, one had crawled on her, causing her to leap and run around like a fool. Another one had decided to search through her handbag and had gone unnoticed until she'd pulled out her wallet at a gas station and it crawled out. No one probably would have noticed if she hadn't jumped back and screamed. Someone had gotten a free Birkin that day with a makeup bag filled with MAC, because she'd refused to take it home with her. She'd walked away with her wallet, more embarrassed than she had ever been in her life. This time, she didn't bring her handbag with her.

"Are you okay?" Gina asked. "Your eyes are puffy. You haven't been crying, have you?"

"Of course not," she replied, trying to straighten her tone. "Decided to stop by to see how you were doing. I hadn't heard from you in a while."

"Oh…" Gina said, putting a coffee filter into a small, white coffeemaker. "I've been busy at the soup kitchen, helping out there."

"That's good." Nikki felt a sliver of happiness that her mother was doing so well.

"Are you sure you're okay?" Gina asked, scooping coffee from a can into the filter.

Nikki exhaled and gave in. "No, Ma. I'm not."

"What's wrong? You're still mad with Duncan, aren't you?" Gina didn't give her a chance to respond. "Now Nikki, I know Duncan had a baby on you and all that, but don't take it out on that baby. Find it in your heart to forgive him."

"What? This coming from you? I thought you didn't like him."

"That's not the point. Honey, it's in men's nature to cheat. They *all* do it," she said with a snort. "I know I don't like him all that much, but I do want what's best for my daughter. You living all fancy over there is a blessing that you shouldn't take for granted."

"I don't," Nikki replied, drying her tears with the back of her hand. "And you may be right, but that's still not what I'm angry about."

"Then what?"

Nikki hesitated before telling her mother but had already decided that she needed to talk to someone about it. And Duncan was not an option. "Well, the other day, I walked in on Rayshad having sex."

"*What?*"

Nikki flinched at her mother's response. "That's not the worst part."

Gina remained silent, waiting.

"He was with…" She closed her eyes. "…a man."

"He was—*what!*" Gina put her hand on her hip. "Something told me—"

"Look, Ma," Nikki said, holding her hands up, "I'm not in the mood for you or anyone else to be throwing anything in my face, right now."

Gina didn't say anything for a minute. "So, what are you going to do?"

"I don't know."

"Well, I'll tell you what you *need* to do. Since he thinks he's so grown that he can disrespect you in your house and that girl Carissa, too, I'd kick him out."

Nikki laughed. "Now that's a bit extreme, don't you think?"

"Hell no. First, he knocks that girl up and now this? He must think he's grown. You can't let the boy do whatever he pleases. Put your foot down!"

Nikki watched a roach crawl across the floor, but tried not to be obvious about seeing it. "I couldn't do that."

"I'll tell you this: I know he's my grandson and all, but I'm through with his ass." Gina threw her hands up and returned to the coffeemaker.

"What?"

"It's an abomination, Nikki! It's in the Word! I'm definitely not gonna stand for it."

Nikki laughed again. "You're kidding, right? You can't give up on Rayshad because of his sexuality."

"Damn straight! That boy is too brilliant to do something like that."

Nikki stood up. "What does being gay have anything to do with brilliance?" Her heart began to race.

"Take it how you want. It's nasty, and if you support him, then…then…I'm done with you, too."

Nikki gasped.

"That's right. I don't play that. My time is limited here. I can't be stressed out about this right now."

"Limited? What do you mean?"

Gina smacked. "Well, actually, I didn't plan on telling you this. At least not before now."

Nikki sat up from the couch and searched her mother. "What, Ma?"

Gina stepped out of the kitchen and sat down next to Nikki. "I have cancer."

"What?"

"And it won't be long."

"Oh, God, Mom!" Nikki slapped her cheek. "When did you find out about this?"

"A couple of months ago."

"And you didn't tell me?"

"For what? To worry you? Or would you even care?"

"Of course I would care!" Nikki shrieked. She leaned over and embraced her mother. "Why wouldn't I? You're my mother. I love you, and I thought you loved me, too." Her lips trembled. "That's why I can't believe you're acting the way you are about this situation. He's your grandson!"

"I don't care. And I'm standing by what I say."

Nikki pulled away. "So you mean to tell me that even with you being sick and all—during a time when we need each other most— you're going to turn your back on me? Again, Mom? Again?"

"If that's how you take it, Nikki. I gave you a choice."

"I can't let that happen, Mom. I'm not about to let go of my son, and I'm not about to let go of you, either!" She started crying, again. "Not like this!" She took a long, slow breath. "What if you don't make it, Ma? Huh?"

Gina didn't say anything.

Nikki shook her head and stood up. "I—I think I should go."

"Fine."

Chapter Twenty-One

Nikki thumped three empty bottles of White Zinfandel on the table and moaned, "Oh, God…" She buried her face in her hands. As lost as she felt, she wondered if God even heard her. Especially since she rarely reached out to Him anymore.

Looking up around the kitchen, she counted exactly a week since she had cooked anything. Half of that week she had spent at the hotel, but since coming back home, she had lost her appetite completely. Duncan was out of town as usual, and Rayshad went out of his way to avoid her. Carissa seemed like she hadn't gotten tired of pizza, yet.

Nikki downed another glass of wine as quickly as she could and poured another, spilling some on the table. She stopped moving when she thought she heard the garage door going up. Was that Rayshad or Duncan? She listened closely and could tell that it was her son. Duncan's car was a lot quieter than Rayshad's Mustang.

All of these years, had she truly been in denial? With it being so sudden, was she wrong now for being upset with his decision to embrace his feminine ways? How long had Rayshad known that he was gay? And what influenced that decision? He damn sure wasn't raised to be that way. Had she done something wrong?

She closed her eyes, reflecting on a time when he was much younger. Maybe she should have put her foot down back when he used to play with Chance's niece and her Barbie dolls. Instead of snapping like Chance did, Nikki would laugh, thinking it was "cute."

And to think that she was number one when it came to pointing fingers at the parent of a disobedient child. "It's what's going on at home that has these children acting like that," she had said to Trina at a church picnic after a girl had just pushed Rayshad to the ground.

"Yeah, but boys will be boys," Trina had replied, stuffing potato salad in her mouth. Looking at Rayshad dusting himself off in his effeminate manner, she had swallowed her food and had added under her breath, "and girls will be girls."

Nikki had caught that. Even though Trina didn't know it, she was never ignorant to everyone thinking Rayshad was gay or would be by the time he grew up. Her heart was so set on proving them wrong that she didn't see it coming.

After polishing off the rest of the wine, she lifted the top of a box of Newports. It had been seven years since she had picked up a cigarette, but on her way home from Gina's, she stopped at a 7-Eleven.

Nikki looked at her lighter and cigarette thinking, *Duncan would kill me if he knew that I smoked in the house.*

She lit it anyway, ignoring the headache that had come from chain smoking three cigarettes before. The last text message she had received from Duncan let her know that he was out of town on business and hoped she would come back home by the time he returned later that evening.

When she looked up, she found Rayshad standing in the doorway, his face crinkled with disgust. "I thought you quit smoking those."

Nikki inhaled her cigarette deeply, ignoring his facial expression. She knew he was obsessive about his health and couldn't stand secondhand smoke, but that was the least of her concerns at the moment.

"And did you drink all three of those?" He eyed the White Zinfandel bottles before her.

Instead of answering his questions, Nikki looked him up and down. "Rayshad, Carissa is about to have your baby. And I'm sorry to say this, son, but I think it's really messed up that you're gay. And I say this from Carissa's point of view. I mean, really..." She leaned over, resting her elbows on the counter. "I was hoping that you would be like your father—marry her, and try to have a family."

Rayshad crossed his arms, avoiding eye contact with her. "I'm really sorry to disappoint you, Ma."

Nikki thought for a moment and nodded. "Disappointed is a good way to describe how I feel right now, yeah. But not even the half, Rayshad." Her voice had gotten louder by the end of the sentence. "Obviously, Carissa doesn't know."

"I'll tell her when the time is right."

Nikki ignored his statement. "And now what? You have a baby on the way."

"Being gay doesn't mean I'm not capable of taking care of a baby."

Nikki narrowed her eyes at Rayshad. "Okay, but do you think this double life of yours is okay?"

Rayshad threw his hands up. "At this point, Ma, I don't care what you or anybody else thinks is appropriate. This is my life! And I've told you before, and I'll say it again! That baby's not mine!"

Nikki gulped when Carissa waddled in and stood by the doorway breathing hard.

Rayshad followed his mother's glance and almost jumped when he saw his girlfriend. His anger melted to guilt as his head fell down.

Carissa looked lost and disappointed at the same time. "Is it true?" she asked Rayshad. "Are you gay?"

Rayshad looked everywhere but at the two women. "Yeah."

"But…but how?" she asked, tears filling her eyes. "I thought you loved me."

Rayshad shoved his hands in his pockets and tilted his head to the side.

"And you don't think this baby is yours, either?" Carissa started breathing hard.

"I don't want to talk about this right now," he said, looking at the ceiling.

"I can't believe my mom was right about you," she cried, pointing her finger at him.

Nikki shook her head, trying best to imagine how Carissa felt but she couldn't. She felt sorry for how she had been misled.

"How could you do this to me?" she cried hysterically, holding the lower part of her stomach. "I'm pregnant with *your* baby, and this is how you do me?" She tried to step forward, but leaned back in pain. She held onto the doorframe and slid to the floor, clutching her belly.

Nikki stood from the table and rushed to Carissa.

"It hurts!" she moaned.

Nikki kneeled down and held the young lady's shoulder. "What, your stomach?"

Carissa nodded.

Nikki looked Carissa over. "Did your water break?"

"I don't know, but I can't take it," she cried, rocking back and forth.

Nikki looked back at Rayshad. "Don't sit there like a bump on a log!"

"What am I supposed to do?" he yelled.

"Dammit, Rayshad, start the car or something! Carissa's about to have this baby!"

"I hate you, Rayshad!" Carissa blurted.

"How was I supposed to know?" he asked his mother, ignoring Carissa.

Nikki hopped up and got in his face. "I'm two seconds away from knocking you out, Rayshad! Do you think

I'm supposed to stick up for you and handle your problems all the time? You are too old for this! You laid up with the girl and had a baby when you knew you were gay, and now, I'm supposed to carry that load for you? Man-up, Rayshad! Man-up!"

Chapter Twenty-Two

Carissa delivered a healthy baby boy after four hours of labor and named him Christopher. Stroking the baby's head softly, Carissa smiled and looked up at her mother.

Margaret sighed. "I wantchu to come back home, now. I may have overreacted a little bit."

"Really, Mom?"

"Yeah." She stroked her daughter's head. "It upset me to see that you were making the same mistake—or following the same path I've gone down. You see how hard I struggle."

Carissa nodded. "I want to come home, Mom. I really do."

A knock at the door interrupted them. Nikki poked her head inside. "Hey," she said, smiling. She had never seen Margaret before but had an idea who the foreign lady was stroking her grandson.

Carissa smiled. "Hey, Ms. Nik."

"I came in to take a peek at the baby before they take him back," she replied, removing her sweater. She shot a look at Margaret. "How are you?"

Margaret's eyes fell to the floor. "Good, and you?"

"Just fine." Nikki stepped forward and held her arms out. "May I?"

Carissa braced herself before handing Christopher to Nikki.

Margaret walked to the other side of the room. "I'm going to step outside and call your brother. He'll help you move your things back home."

As the door shut behind Margaret, Nikki looked at Carissa. She really didn't blame her for wanting to go back home.

"I can't believe he's gay," Carissa said quietly. "Why didn't you tell me, Ms. Nik?"

Nikki sighed. "I just found out myself."

"I know, but...he's *gay!* I didn't want to be with a *gay* man. I don't want to have a baby by a *gay* man!" she cried out. "And...and I knew he was acting funny about me being pregnant. I wish he would've told me he didn't think it was his. Ms. Nik, I swear I wouldn't be here if I knew he felt that way."

Nikki rocked the baby back and forth. She always knew her son was going to be a heartbreaker, but she never envisioned that it would be for this reason. "Carissa, I'm just as shocked as you. And I told you before that even if you don't have anyone else on your team—my son included—I am."

Carissa looked the other way.

❧ ❧ ❧

Rayshad locked eyes on the baby through a window at the hospital and sighed. Duncan watched the teenager staring hopelessly and couldn't believe that his stepson was really a father.

"The baby's so little and cute," Rayshad said, looking back at Duncan. "I didn't think I'd be feeling this way about it when I saw him."

"Yeah, babies are precious," Duncan replied. The more time he spent with his daughter, Kenya, the more he regretted not being there for her from the start. "But, if you think the baby's not yours…" he pried.

Rayshad looked up at Duncan. "Can I?"

Duncan put his hand on Rayshad's back. He wanted to know if the baby was his as badly as Rayshad. "Of course."

A door closing shut prompted Duncan to turn around and find Nikki exiting Carissa's room up the hallway. When she looked up and saw him there, she took a deep breath and swiftly moved toward the elevator. "Nikki, wait!"

She pressed a button on the wall and the elevator opened. As the doors were closing, Duncan put his foot between them, causing them to pop back open. He stepped inside even though Nikki's crossed arms told him that she did not want him to.

"Will you please talk to me, Nikki? Please?"

"I don't have anything to say to you."

He held her arms despite her resistance. "Well, I do."

"Too bad I don't want to hear it." She shuffled away from him. "Let me go."

Duncan stepped back and opened his mouth to speak, but did not know where to begin. "I saw your things in the guest room when I got back from my trip today."

Nikki didn't say anything.

"I missed you," he said more like an apology than an announcement. "I made a mistake, Nikki. I admit that. And I promise you I'll never do it again. Just give me the opportunity to make it up to you."

The elevator stopped moving and the doors opened.

"Let's do something together," he suggested. "Take a trip. Go to the islands. We can renew our vows."

"A trip sounds like a good idea," Nikki said.

Duncan blinked, almost surprised by her response, and smiled. "We can go anywhere you want, baby. Name a place."

Nikki stepped outside of the elevator. "Anywhere but here." She looked him up and down, her arms still crossed. "And with anyone but you."

He sighed hopelessly.

Nikki glared at Duncan so intensely that when she walked away to the parking lot, he chose not to follow behind.

Chapter Twenty-Three

C hance and Nikki walked out of Bally's laughing and holding hands. Walking up the Las Vegas strip, they marveled over the 25th annual Donn Arden's Jubilee show they had just attended.

As much as he had been dying to gamble since dinner, Chance had to admit that the seven-act production was spectacular. Wowed by the beautiful dancers, glitzy costumes, and robust musical numbers, he couldn't keep his eyes off of the stage. Gorgeous women adorned in fancy oversized feathers and sparkly rhinestones swayed across the smoky million-dollar set, costumes designed by Bob Mackie. The special effects had the entire crowd amazed, and at the end, everyone offered a standing ovation.

Out of nowhere, Chance grabbed Nikki by the face and sucked her lips softly. Nikki's body tingled as she was gifted with a tantalizing kiss. When Chance pulled away, she was speechless.

He still held her cheeks, looking into her eyes. "Thank you," he whispered.

Nikki parted her lips to catch her breath.

"I really do love you."

Her stomach fluttered. She pressed her lips together and swallowed. Wrapping her arms around Chance, a tear fell from her eye. She wiped it away before he noticed.

"You know, I never in a million years thought that we would divorce," he said.

"Me neither."

"And, I'm still tripping off the fact that Rayshad got some chick pregnant."

"Yeah." Nikki wondered if updating Chance on Rayshad's life was such a good idea. She still had not told him that Rayshad was gay.

Not yet.

They continued walking down the dark sidewalk. He vaguely heard footsteps behind them, but didn't think much of them. It was a beautiful night so they couldn't be the only ones out for a stroll.

"Is he going to make an honest woman out of her and marry her?" Chance asked.

"They aren't even together anymore," Nikki replied.

"Oh?"

"But that's another story we'll talk about later."

Chance turned to see who had crept up behind them.

"Well, well…what have we here?"

Two dirty, smelly men stepped in their direction. One of them spat on the ground and cracked his knuckles. "Two lovebirds, eh?"

Unprepared, Chance braced himself and thought of his next move. He maneuvered his body in front of Nikki's.

The last brawl he had been involved in was back in college when his roommate had found out he was dating Nikki. He didn't back down then, and he wasn't backing down now.

They laughed—a stench collectively worse than their body odors put together. "Check this man out," one with a missing tooth spat.

"You don't want no trouble," Chance warned, looking back and forth between the two of them. "Trust me." He grabbed Nikki's hand and looked them up and down. "Come on, baby. Let's go." They made an attempt to step around the men who smelled of piss and booze.

"I don't think so." The toothless man stepped forward and blocked their path. A knife whipped out of his hand, causing Chance to flinch.

He prepared himself for battle. "Move back, Nikki." He bit his bottom lip and braced himself to throw the first punch. Never had he fought more than one person at a time and he didn't have a strategy, but the last thing he was going to do was show them how terrified he really was.

Suddenly, their laughter faded and faces melted. The two men walked backward in horror.

They were more cowardly than Chance had thought. But when he paid closer attention, they weren't backing away in fear from him. He turned around and gasped.

"Back up!" Nikki yelled. Her arms were stretched forward, hands gripped firmly around a pistol.

Chance's jaw dropped as then men backed away.

She cocked the hammer and moved forward. "Get out of here before I put a bullet in both of you!"

"Okay, lady," said the toothless leader. "It's cool, it's cool." He and his buddy's hands were high in the air.

Chance's mouth opened to speak. There were so many questions to ask Nikki, but no time to talk. Bringing a gun to a knife fight was a definite end to all brawls, but where had she gotten it from? And why was she carrying it with her? He looked at Nikki's small, petite frame and never would have imagined her pulling this kind of move.

He turned back to the two rogues who were steady backing away. "Well?" he said more boldly.

They clumsily skipped away.

"Come on," Nikki said, tucking the weapon back in her oversized clutch. "Let's go."

They walked as fast as they could toward the next casino.

Chance's heart was still racing when the muggers were finally out of sight. "What the hell was that?" he asked.

"Tell me about it."

"I meant the gun." He used both of his hands to wipe his perspiring face. "And I'm glad you had it, but why the hell are you carrying it?"

"My husband bought it for me," she said, shrugging her shoulders.

"Your husband?" Chance said dryly. Even though his pride had taken its own beating at the fact that a woman had saved his life, he was glad they both got away safely.

Nikki was a lot tougher than she used to be, and her new mate could take the credit.

"Why are you carrying it with you in your purse?"

Nikki blinked. "Because…" she said quietly, a cold look in her eyes. "You never know what might happen."

Chills ran through his body and it wasn't from the cool breeze sweeping over him.

"Especially here in Sin City."

Chapter Twenty-Four

Duncan took another swig of whiskey and slammed the bottle down next to the death threat he'd carried around with him all night. He stared at the note as he wiped the stinging liquor from his lips with the back of his hand.

The note had haunted him since he'd received it hours ago, and the message was pretty clear. But no matter how far his mind stretched, he couldn't put his finger on any particular person who wanted him dead.

Since Nikki had lied about being at her mother's, then had the nerve to hang up on him, Duncan was done trying to get in touch with her. She would come home eventually.

He had a proposal for a $35 million deal due on Monday. Marie wouldn't stop hounding him about Demetria—a child she didn't want him to have anything to do with. But now, since he was worth more money, she wanted him to "see" his daughter.

For the past hour, he had tried to focus his attention on the computer screen—almost an impossible task with the many distracting things rumbling through his thoughts. The whiskey wasn't helping his concentration, either.

His marriage was falling down the drain; a man who didn't deserve Nikki to begin with was winning her back over; and to top all of it off, someone had a hit out on him. How could he care about a proposal at a time like this? Money came too easy for him to worry about a deal when so many things in his personal life were at stake. But he grabbed the keyboard and mouse anyhow.

Clicking the Internet icon, a browser window opened. He typed the address of a property into a database, and when hitting "submit," a disturbing pop-up appeared out of nowhere.

Duncan's mouth dropped.

Two bare-chested men holding one another stood beside bold letters soliciting free videos and picture galleries. He clicked the red X button to close the advertisement. Where did that come from? Their computer had annoying pop-ups every now and then, but never from a pornographic site. A gay one at that.

Only one person in their house would probably want to view something like that.

There was nothing Nikki could say to convince Duncan that her son didn't have gay tendencies. He was willing to bet that, even if she walked in on Rayshad with his mouth on another man's penis, she would come up with an excuse for that, too. If only his wife had sense enough to know better.

Duncan paused as another thought hit him. He scrolled through the Internet browser's recent history. The pointer swiped across various URLs as he looked for any sites that alluded to explicit content.

Several Vegas tourist sites had been visited in the past couple of days. He clicked on each link, and was guided to a reservation page.

Grabbing the whiskey bottle, he poured himself another glass while staring at Bally's website. He took another gulp of liquor, picked up a pen, and started jotting down phone numbers. A gut feeling led him to believe that he was on to something.

When he polished off the last of his drink, he punched the first set of numbers.

"Thank you for calling—"

"Can you connect me to Nikki Johnson's room, please?"

"Hold, please."

Duncan heard a click and his heart raced as the jazz hold music played in the background.

Moments later, the music stopped. "Sir?"

"Yes."

"I could not locate a Nikki Johnson."

"Thanks." He hung up the phone and sat back in his seat. After giving the phone a wary stare, something clicked into place. His wife was never the type to pay for anything. The room had to be in Chance's name!

He dialed a second time.

"Thank you for calling—"

"Can you please connect me to Chance Brown's room, please?"

"Hold, please."

Duncan's toe tapped rapidly against the hardwood floor as he waited for the call to connect. Had he finally caught her?

"Sir?" said the front desk receptionist.

"Yes," he replied.

"I am now connecting you to Chance Brown's room."

Duncan's stomach dipped, but instead of staying on the line, he disconnected the call and set the cordless down.

An overnight getaway in Vegas? Things were worse than he suspected. Nikki *was* having an affair. How the hell did she think she could get away with staying out all night? Was this what she was doing when she had disappeared for several days after finding out about Marie a month ago?

Downing the rest of the liquor, he stood. "Over my dead body."

Dead body.

Dead.

YOU WILL DIE AND YOU KNOW WHY.

Storming to the bedroom, he threw open his closet door and dove in to find a wooden box hidden behind a stack of shoeboxes. He pried it open to grab his gun, but fell back against the closet wall and gripped his chest.

His .32 was there, but Nikki's pistol wasn't.

Duncan's mind soared with images of Nikki making

plans to kill him, so she could take his money, then ride off into the sunset with Chance.

"I'll be damned," he whispered.

Duncan tucked his gun in his pants and raced downstairs. In less than thirty seconds flat, he was in his car headed to the freeway.

Chapter Twenty-Five

C hance couldn't finish pressing the button before Nikki slid her soft body against his and started kissing his neck. Once the elevator doors closed, he leaned her against the wall, wrapped her thigh around him, and caught her sweet, supple lips with his. As their tongues slowly danced with one another, the stiffness in his pants pressed against her pelvis, threatening to ravish her right there. But when the doors opened, she moved his hand from under her dress and pulled him down the hallway to their room.

Chance let go of her grasp and allowed her to walk far in front him, so he could watch her prance up the hallway. He loved how her hips moved from side to side, and in a minute, would be pulling them back to him.

When Nikki slid the keycard into the slot and pushed the door open, he removed his jacket and sat at the edge of the bed. He reached both of his hands underneath her dress as she stood above him, but she stepped back and smiled.

"I'm about to change into something more comfortable. Okay?"

"You do that," he replied, propping back on his elbows.

He studied her bottom as she walked away, switching from side to side. When the bathroom door closed, he hopped up and anxiously undressed down to his boxers.

Finally. Nikki was where he wanted her ever since she had come back in his life. Of course he had tried to get it other times, but she never had accepted his advances.

Not until tonight.

He plopped back on the bed and laid his head in the palms of clasped hands. Closing his heavy eyes, he envisioned slipping inside of her. He wondered if her favorite position was still riding on top. That would be perfect for him to view her new breasts. He couldn't wait to touch, squeeze, and kiss them.

He opened one of his eyes enough to see the clock across the room. 1:02 a.m. As he closed his eye to envision what kind of lingerie Nikki was putting on for him, nausea began simmering in his stomach. He tried counting how many drinks he'd had that night but he had difficulty focusing.

Suddenly, there was an aggressive knock at the front door.

He jumped. *Who could that be?*

Chance pulled himself up from the bed, wondering if he had heard correctly. Neither he or Nikki ordered room service, but with everything she had already surprised him with, he wondered if this could have been the best yet.

Or could it be...

Chance stopped dead in his tracks as his fiancée, Olivia, crossed his mind. Was it possible that she knew what was going on? She was becoming insecure all over again since she had found a few phone numbers in his cell phone, but was she crazy enough to trace him all the way to Vegas? He shook the paranoia away. She hadn't called him all night, and when Olivia was upset, she usually called him repeatedly.

Rapid knocking from the front door echoed throughout the room. Chance hesitated again, looking back at the bathroom door. Did Nikki cover *her* tracks enough to prevent her husband from following her? They were too far away for anyone to know anything. But the closer he approached the door, the more he sensed that something wasn't right.

Chance twisted the knob, opened the door, and gasped. Terror gripped him by the throat when he blinked at the person before him. A tanned blonde with a striking resemblance to Olivia made him jump.

"Oops." She laughed and looked Chance up and down. "I think I have the wrong room." She giggled sheepishly as her eyes landed on his black boxers.

Chance closed the door, blowing a sigh of relief. He held his stomach as he stumbled back to the bed. His heart was still beating fast and the nausea began bubbling worse than before. What was he so worried about? This was the best evening he had enjoyed in years.

Click.

Chance lifted up from among the pillows the moment Nikki walked out of the bathroom.

He shot up. "What the—?"

The barrel of a gun was pointed inches away from his face. He looked between Nikki's face and her hands gripping the weapon.

"What the hell?"

Chapter Twenty-Six

Duncan pressed down on the gas, racing up the highway. The shooting range was closed, so what else was there for him to do? Simply drive. Drive and see where the road would take him.

After giving her the world, this was how she repaid him?

Were both of them in on it? Duncan had heard of people doing anything for the love of money. Nikki would be the sole beneficiary of his multimillion-dollar insurance policy. Maybe that had been the plan all along—marry him, kill him and get rich. Chance may have been a successful attorney, but he had nowhere near the kind of money Duncan had.

For an hour Duncan wandered aimlessly until he realized how close he was to Nikki's old neighborhood in Bel Air. The idea of driving by Chance's home popped into his mind until it dawned on him that there was no use. Chance was in Las Vegas having the time of his life. But a few minutes later, he found himself parked outside of Nikki's old home questioning his sanity.

"What the hell am I doing here?" He reached over to

the passenger's seat and screwed the cap off of an unopened whiskey bottle. He looked at the label before taking a swig. "You're a drunk fool, you know that?"

He stared at the all-white, two-story home before him, taking in the small chandelier he could see through the window over the two French doors.

"I might be a drunk fool, but I'll be damned if I be a dead one."

He stumbled out of his car and made his way up to the front porch, patting his pocket for the gun. A few seconds after chiming the doorbell, he heard chatter from the other side of the door.

Duncan kept his hand in his pocket.

"Who is it?" a feminine voice called.

The door cracked open and he leaned to the side to get a better view. All he could make out was a light-skinned woman with long blonde hair.

"Can I help you?" she asked with an attitude.

"Yeah...I was wondering if Chance was home."

"No, he's not."

"He's not?"

The woman opened the door all the way. "Why? Who are you?"

He stepped back, not expecting her to be so tall. She had to stand at least six feet with long legs and big breasts, dressed in a silk robe that touched her toes.

"My name is Duncan. I'm—"

"Nikki's husband," Olivia said, looking him over suspiciously. "Chance's ex-wife. I know who you are." She looked him over while he did the same. "Well, what do you want? What are you doing here?"

"Well…" Even in his drunken stupor, reality set in. Coming here was a big mistake. "I might as well tell you," he mumbled. "I came here because I have suspicions that my wife's fooling around with your husband."

Her eyes narrowed. "Why do you think that?" She flung the door open and stormed back inside the house, expecting him to follow. "Come in!"

Duncan stepped inside, shoving his hands into his pockets. He looked around the two-story home to confirm that it was as nice a home as his, but Nikki definitely had upgraded when they had moved to Beverly Hills.

Olivia thumbed through a pack of cigarettes, reminding him that Nikki had smelled of smoke lately.

Olivia lit her cigarette, took a deep pull, and let the smoke drizzle from her nose. "So what's the story?" she mumbled, staring at an object across the room.

"Well…"

"I *knew* he was cheating on me again!" Olivia blurted before Duncan could fill her in on why he suspected the affair. "He comes in late and hasn't been answering his phone lately!"

Duncan opened his mouth to speak, but Olivia popped up out of her seat and marched out of the room.

"Can I get you something to drink?" she yelled from the kitchen.

"You got any liquor?" Duncan asked, as though he hadn't hit a neighbor's mailbox before he got there.

She popped her head out of the kitchen and gestured to an area off to the left. "A whole bar."

"Maker's Mark on the rocks."

Olivia returned minutes later with a red drink for herself and held out his. Her nails were long as claws.

"This news...it hurts, because we're supposed to be getting married in a couple of weeks. Everything's set." She sipped her drink. "Well, except the groom."

Duncan nodded.

"I had no idea that he was still messing around with that bitch!" She glanced at Duncan, but didn't seem to care whether she offended him or not.

"Messed me up, too."

"So, what clued you in?" She crossed one long leg over the other and flexed her toes.

Duncan took a big gulp of his drink. "She's been acting strange lately, so I checked out her cell phone bill and saw she'd been calling Chance several times a day." As Duncan tipped back the smooth whisky, he felt his high increase even more.

Olivia looked at Duncan for a long moment and then laughed. "That's it?"

"Hell, she lied and said she was at her mother's, but when I called her mom, she said that she hadn't heard from her in weeks." Duncan blinked when Olivia's face began to look familiar to him. "And that's been Nikki's excuse lately...that she's been at her *mom's* house."

Olivia sat up and pursed her lips. "And what's that got to do with Chance?"

"Just putting two and two together."

"And coming up with ten." Olivia laughed. "Well, I'm sorry, honey, but I need more proof than that. I thought you had a real reason to suspect they were cheating. With that said…" She stood up and set her drink down. "I think you need to go. My man should be home any minute, and the last thing I need is for him to catch another man in his house a couple of weeks before our wedding." She stood at the front door, waiting for Duncan to follow suit.

Duncan didn't move. "I *guarantee* you he's not on the way."

Olivia crossed her arms. "And why wouldn't he be?"

"Just do this one thing." He pulled his cell phone out of his back pocket.

She slowly walked toward him. "What?"

"Call this number." He scrolled to the digits, then held out his phone after the search.

She snatched the phone. "And what's this?"

"It's the number to the Las Vegas hotel where they're staying."

Olivia's forehead crinkled as she stared at the phone. "What-ever."

"Call and ask them to connect you to his room," he instructed.

She smirked as she dialed the number. Putting the phone to her ear, she stared at Duncan. "Hi, can you connect me to Chance Brown's room, please?"

Duncan observed the conversation, while sipping on the rest of his drink.

Olivia's eyebrows rose. "I know she did *not* just put me on hold! I know she is *not* about to transfer me to Chance, because I *know* that Chance is *not* in Vegas!"

Duncan shrugged and looked out of the window, noticing a dent in the front of his car from hitting the mailbox.

"They're connecting me to the room right now," she whispered, eyes widening to the size of yolks. "I swear to God, if Chance answers this phone—"

Olivia didn't finish her sentence, but Duncan had a good idea of what Olivia was capable of doing. She appeared more aggressive than his own wife, whom he still suspected was behind the plot to murder him.

After a minute, Olivia became fed up and pressed a button that disconnected the call.

"No answer?" Duncan asked.

Olivia shoved the phone back in his hand. "Oh no he didn't! What the hell is he doing in Vegas? And with *that* bitch?"

She downed the rest of her drink and stormed off toward the bar.

Chapter Twenty-Seven

C hance shook his head and gawked at Nikki. She was looking sexy as hell in her red and black corset with garter belts and fishnets, but why did she have a gun to his face? He held his hands as high up as they could go, his eyes wide and confused. "What's going on?"

"Shut up!" Nikki screamed. She stood in front of Chance, gripping the gun like a pro. "You deserve this shit, and you know it."

His eyes narrowed as he searched Nikki's sexy body dressed in lingerie. "This ain't some kinky dominatrix shit, is it? 'Cause I can tell you right now that my dick went from ten inches to soft instantly."

Nikki pressed her lips together. "Don't flatter yourself! It was never that big to begin with."

"Come on, man! You can't be serious."

"Want to try me?"

"I should've known your crazy ass was up to something!"

Nikki laughed menacingly. "I'd watch my mouth if I were you. Only a fool would talk crazy with a gun in his face."

"Then what the hell is this about? It's been seven years, Nikki! Seven years! And you coming for me, *now?*"

"You damned right I am!"

"After all you took me through, Nikki—man—come on, now. I thought we called it even with the alimony!"

"We *still* won't be even well after you're dead and gone."

"Man, I can't believe this," he moaned, wiping his face with his hand.

"Well, believe it. Because this is real."

Chance tried to look away, but the gun kept his attention. "I don't know why you're tripping like this! That Trina shit is old. Your ass moved on to another man real quick, and you still feel like you have something to prove?"

"Forget about Trina!"

"Look, I'm sorry for sleeping with your best friend, but shit, we've both moved on with our lives. After Trina told me Rayshad wasn't mine, I didn't come for you! This shit is foul."

"She's not the reason you're about to take one to the head." Her eyes tightened. "You did something that cut me to the core. Hardcore, like for real. And Chance…" She pressed the gun a mere inch from his forehead. "You know *exactly* what I'm talking about."

Nikki spooned lobster bisque flambé from the large pot and sipped it. "Mmm…" She hadn't cooked for over two weeks, and this one tasted better than the shrimp bisque her mother initially refused to taste, but ended up loving. She reached for the Sherry wine and poured a little bit more across the top.

A door closed at a distance. Nikki looked at the clock and hoped Rayshad had walked in instead of Duncan, who was still the last person she wanted to see. He planned to pick his daughter up on the way home from work—the third time he had gotten her since Marie had popped up.

Rayshad walked into the kitchen with a frown and sad eyes. An envelope was in his hand.

The child must be his, she thought. She knew he wasn't thrilled about the responsibility while being tied to a woman who practically hated him now.

"So, what's it say?" she asked, reaching for the results.

Rayshad smirked. "I told you."

Nikki skimmed through the paper, before stopping at

the bold print. The results were 99.9 percent accurate, and Rayshad *was not* the father.

"Oh…" Nikki held her chest and walked with her son to the living room. They sat down on the couch, and she rubbed his head. His disappointment touched her, because she thought he would be relieved. She briefly wondered what Carissa was going through at that moment.

"The bright side of the situation is that you didn't want the responsibility," Nikki said after a few moments. "So I guess in some kind of way, this is a blessing."

Rayshad looked the other way. "Yeah, but I still wanted to believe her, though."

Nikki understood his bitterness. She was a bit upset that Carissa had used them for a place to stay after getting knocked up by some other man and kicked out by her angry mother.

Rayshad shrugged. "I don't know. I really didn't want to have the baby, but at the same time, I knew that would probably be my only chance at having a kid."

Nikki stopped rubbing Rayshad's head. Statements like that reconfirmed what she tried so hard to forget. She placed her hand on his shoulder. "No more girlfriends, then, okay?" She smiled warmly as she rubbed her son's back. "I don't need you breaking no other girl's heart."

Rayshad smiled.

Nikki knew he was surprised that she didn't have anything negative to say.

"I won't," he said.

"Don't be disappointed, Rayshad. We all make mistakes. Carissa is only human like you."

"She's the one who has an attitude with *me*."

"Can you really blame her?" Nikki knew if she found out Duncan were gay, she would go haywire. What woman could accept her man being an undercover brother?

"I guess not," he replied, tilting his head, "but still…"

Nikki shook her head. "You'll learn."

He dismissed her statement with a wave of his hand. "Whatever, Ma."

"I'm serious. You can't go around hurting people, not caring about how they feel."

"I didn't do it on purpose."

"Watch it, because everything you do to others will come back on you." She thought about Marie and Demetria. "Then one day when you get hurt or experience certain situations, you wonder what you've done in life to deserve these things, and—"

"I know all about karma, Ma. I know."

As Rayshad rambled on, Nikki was still thinking about Duncan's affair and compared the mistakes she had made early in her marriage with Chance. She was going to have to forgive Duncan sooner or later. Chance had raised Rayshad as his own because of mistakes she had made.

"I'm glad this situation is over with," he continued. "I can go on with my life."

"I want to tell you something," Nikki said, scooting

closer to him. "I've been wanting to tell you for a long time when the time was right, and now I think it is."

He gave his mother a curious look. "What?"

"Well," Nikki said, wringing her fingers. She looked down but back up at his eyes again. "I made a mistake a *looooong* time ago. A mistake similar to Carissa's."

Rayshad's eyes widened as if he knew what Nikki was going to say.

"I…" Nikki looked up and rubbed a trembling hand over her thigh. "How should I say this?" She grabbed his hand, needing it more than he needed hers. "In a nutshell, your father, Chance…" She swallowed the large lump in her throat. "He really *isn't* your father."

His eyes couldn't get any bigger, so his mouth dropped. "You're joking, right?"

Nikki felt a sense of relief unveiling the secret she had been holding in for so long. Rayshad deserved to know who his real father was. "I'm sorry that I didn't tell you sooner."

Rayshad jumped to his feet. "I can't believe this!"

Nikki took a deep breath and tried to come up with something that could smooth the situation over, while bracing herself for any questions he might have.

"Why did you wait so long to tell me?" His arms flailed aggressively by his sides. "All of this time, Ma?"

"I know," Nikki said quietly. "But, the way things happened. It—it just—"

Think of something. A lie. Anything!

"Chance was a good man." She rolled her eyes. "He was willing to raise you as his own child even though you weren't his. And we should both be thankful for that."

"Thankful?" Rayshad yelled. "All the things Chance put me through and I should be *thankful?*"

Nikki wondered if she had made the right decision telling him. Her heart melted when she looked up and saw him standing at the window with his arms crossed. Half of his body was shadowed by the tall bookshelf beside him.

"I'm sorry for getting angry like that," he said softly.

Nikki's eyebrows shot up, expecting that to be the last thing he would say. She blinked several times and stood up. "No. *I'm* sorry."

Rayshad closed his eyes, holding up his hand. "No. No." Taking a deep breath, he looked away. "We've *both* been holding a lot of secrets in all these years."

Nikki slightly turned her head, afraid of what he was about to uncover. What other secret could he be holding on to after she'd found out about his true sexuality?

"Like you, I wanted to wait until the right time..."

She shook her head and forced a smile. "What?"

Rayshad took a deep breath. "Sometimes this man would come into my room at night." He cringed before moving forward. "Do things to me and make me touch him. Make me do things that I wasn't comfortable with." His voice trembled. "Made me promise not to tell you, or he would kill you."

Nikki's mouth dropped open as her thoughts ran through all types of scenarios. "You're not saying that man was Chance, are you?"

Rayshad hesitated, looked up at his mother, and blinked back a tear.

Nikki gripped the edge of the couch and saw red. "That motherfucker!"

৵ ৵ ৵

"Have you ever sucked a dick, Chance?" Nikki asked, pushing her gun in his mouth. The metal clicked against his teeth, as he lay sprawled on the bed. "Would you have been turned on if I let you fuck me in the ass and sport a strap-on? I mean, you're a sick man. For real. Not only are you this undercover brother, but you rape kids, and a kid you *thought* was yours."

Beads of perspiration danced across Chance's forehead as his brown skin grew red and his chest heaved up and down. His face crinkled as he tried to mumble with the gun in his mouth.

"I know I wasn't perfect in our relationship," Nikki went on. "Not by a long shot. But this takes the cake."

Yanking the gun from his mouth, she slowly walked across the room. "You destroyed our son, Chance! He was perfectly fine until you abused him." She stopped walking and held her face with one hand and her back turned away from him. "Did you know that he's gay now,

Chance? Huh? Not undercover like you, but full-blown gay!" She wiped her face. "When I first found out, I blamed myself. I tried to figure out where I went wrong and—"

Before Nikki could turn around all the way, Chance lunged at her, tackling her to the ground. Knocking her grip loose, the gun slid across the floor as he fell on top of her. She squeezed his neck with both of her hands while trying to maneuver her body from underneath him.

Chance suddenly jerked to the side, giving her the opportunity to push him off of her. She crawled across the floor, grabbed the gun, and rolled over. As she was about to aim for him, his body continued jerking uncontrollably. She lowered the gun, stood up, and backed away. A few seconds later, his convulsions stopped.

Chance lay motionless with his eyes and mouth wide open. She swallowed and stared at the body for a couple of minutes before slowly walking toward him. "Chance?" She stood several feet from him and held her breath.

Had the poison worked?

His glazed eyes stared at her for several minutes without blinking. No part of his body moved to signal breathing. She took three steps forward and kneeled down slowly, afraid that he might pop up at any moment.

Chance was dead.

She dropped the gun and stumbled back into a chair in the corner of the room. No matter how many deep breaths she took, her heart steadily beat against her chest like it wanted to bust. She reached for her clutch and pulled out a cigarette. Her hand shook as she made several attempts to flick the lighter.

The longer Nikki stared at the stiff body, the more she couldn't believe that she actually had gone through with it. She hated Chance for what he had done to Rayshad and believed he deserved his fate, but seeing her ex lying on the floor lifeless confused her mixed emotions. This was a man who used to be her husband. The only other man she loved with all her heart. What had she done?

Nikki shook her remorseful thoughts away and forced herself to see it for what it really was. Chance had abused Rayshad and had turned him into something that he would have never been, so he had it coming.

Crushing the cigarette butt in an ashtray, she took a deep breath and stood up. As Nikki approached the corpse, she looked around the room and realized that her job was only half finished.

"And you know what's so messed up?" she said, kneeling over Chance as if he were still alive. "You didn't even deny it."

Chapter Twenty-Nine

Duncan gave one last pump and pushed Olivia's hips forward over the arm of the couch. She continued to lean over even though he had stepped back. He glanced at his pants, crumpled at his ankles, and looked back at her round butt. She turned to look in his eyes as they both tried to catch their breaths.

"That was good," Olivia said, standing tall. She adjusted her nightgown that they had never removed and reached for her drink on the coffee table.

"Yeah. I thought so, too," he replied between breaths. He looked down and felt foolish still dressed in his shirt and his legs exposed. "Do you have a towel or something?"

Olivia pointed to an area behind him. "In the bathroom."

Duncan struggled to keep his pants up as he maneuvered up the hallway past the kitchen. As the water ran over his hands, he looked at his reflection. He expected to feel some kind of satisfaction for fucking Chance's fiancée since he was with his wife, but he felt empty. And that still didn't solve the mystery behind the death threat.

He returned to the living room to find Olivia sitting on the couch smoking a cigarette. She eyed him, but looked away quickly. An uncomfortable silence followed.

"Do you feel better?" she asked, flicking the cigarette.

Duncan turned her direction but couldn't look at her.

She puffed the cigarette. "I mean, about Nikki cheating on you with my fiancé and all."

He shook his head.

Olivia blew smoke in another direction. "This isn't Chance's first time cheating on me," she said. "I don't know why he won't be faithful. I've never cheated. Not before tonight." She looked up at Duncan. "What about you?"

"Two years into our marriage I had a brief affair. Got the woman pregnant and Nikki found out about it a month ago."

"Really?" Olivia asked in a peculiar way. "Damn." She inhaled her cigarette. "Is that what this is all about? You think she's fooling around because of what she found out?"

"Yeah." He looked her over. "Kind of like what you're doing to Chance right now."

She smirked and looked away.

"Is the wedding still on?"

Olivia's eyes looked up in thought. "I don't know."

"Is there really anything to think about?" he asked.

She shook her head. "I don't know."

The clock on the wall ticked through their silence.

"The sad thing is: this isn't the only thing I'm finding out about him."

"Yeah?"

Olivia smacked. "I recently walked in on him snorting coke." She shook her head. "All this time he's been doing it right up under my nose."

Duncan patted his thigh. "Well, there's your answer."

Olivia rolled her eyes into another subject. "I guess you have a lot to think about, too."

"Not really," he replied. "I've been thinking about it all night."

"And?"

Duncan put his hand in his pocket in search of his keys. "And I…I think I better be going."

Her eyes narrowed at him as she stood. Without saying anything more, she escorted him to the door.

Duncan walked past Olivia and stopped. A kiss would not have been appropriate, so he moved on. "Thanks," he replied, not knowing if he was referring to the drink, talk, or sex. As soon as he stepped outside, she closed the door behind him.

The cool breeze swept over him as he walked to his car. He wasn't as drunk as when he'd arrived, but he had almost forgotten about the dent in his car and cursed when he saw it.

Pulling out of the driveway, Duncan questioned whether he should return home. He didn't feel safe with both Nikki and her gun missing. Obviously she was up to something.

Olivia was right. He still had a lot to think about.

Chapter Thirty

Unzipping her luggage, Nikki pulled out a black, long-sleeved jumpsuit. Dressing quickly, she kept looking back at the bed where she had repositioned the body. It had taken a lot longer than she had thought, because she had never imagined him being so heavy. She had closed his eyes, so he looked as if he had fallen asleep while sitting up against the headboard. The comforter covered his bottom half.

Her heart rate still hadn't slowed to normal. She sifted through her bag and searched a zippered compartment. The latex gloves were still on her hands since moving the corpse. Once she located the plastic bag she was looking for, she darted to the restroom.

You'll get away with this, she reassured herself. *Just do everything right.* Snatching a face towel from the sink, she noticed that her hands were still shaking. She ran water over the cloth and went back to the bed and started wiping Chance down. The dresser next. Then the wineglasses. The doorknob, out and in. She only touched things that were absolutely necessary, so only a minimal amount of fingerprints and DNA would linger. Then she followed suit in the bathroom.

Before packing up and making her exit, she pulled a bag of cocaine and a small mirror from the plastic bag. Grabbing his hand, she pressed his fingertips against them, then used the drugs to make a couple of lines on the small mirror and placed it in his lap. Stepping back, her eyes analyzed every aspect of the set-up. She hoped this would work.

Glancing at Chance one last time, her lip trembled. "I'm sorry," she whispered. Tears fell down her cheeks and before she knew it, she was bawling, breaking down to her knees. Wiping her eyes, she pulled herself up, kissed her hand and waved it in his direction.

She didn't take the gloves off until she made it into the hallway.

Nikki walked with such urgency down the hotel corridor that she had to remind herself to slow down so she wouldn't draw attention. Blinking, she realized that she did not have on her shades.

Dammit! How did she forget? Dropping her luggage, she fumbled through her handbag. There they were.

"Excuse me, Miss?"

Nikki's heart skipped a beat. Ignoring the lady with a thick Mexican accent, she picked up her bags and darted toward the elevator.

"Miss!" the lady called out. "You dropped 'dis!"

Nikki's feet stopped moving. She turned to find a short lady walking up to her with her hand outstretched.

"You need 'dis?" she asked, presenting a latex glove.

Nikki laughed nervously and quickly grabbed it from her. "Trash," she said, balling it up. How could she be so careless?

She stepped onto the elevator, still horrified. First, she forgot to put on her shades. Then she almost lost a vital piece of evidence. Taking several deep breaths, she assured herself that everything was fine.

The elevator doors opened and she sped toward the parking garage. Her heels clicked against the pavement as she scurried through the dimly lit area. Was anyone watching her? Suddenly, she heard footsteps echoing at a distance. No one should have been after her, but it sure felt like it. She spotted her Corvette and ran.

In a hurry, Nikki fumbled with her keys trying to unlock the door and dropped them. "Get it together, Nikki," she mumbled. When she finally got in the car, she was out of breath. *But no one knows*, she kept reminding herself. No one could be after her.

Closing her eyes, she tried to convince herself to be happy that her mission was accomplished. *God, I know I was wrong, but please let this work*, she prayed. As she turned the key in the ignition, she eyed the glowing clock. 2:01 a.m. She pulled the Corvette out of the parking garage and headed home.

On to her final mission.

Chapter Thirty-One

Speeding up the highway with the top down, the breeze picked up Nikki's hair like a cape flying in the wind. Even though it was cold, Nikki needed the fresh air. It seemed to calm her down better than a cigarette.

"What the hell did I do?" she cried, beating the steering wheel. The road became a blur; her eyes were so flooded with tears.

"But he deserved it!" she continued to convince herself. "He had no right."

But nothing she said or thought made her feel better. Why was she feeling so bad?

Suddenly, bright red and blue lights illuminated behind her. She shot a look at her rearview mirror as her heart leapt from her chest. A police car swiftly approached her from a distance.

Terror gripped Nikki in every part of her body. What the hell was she supposed to do now? Did they know? Was this connected to Chance's murder?

Couldn't be.

Nikki didn't take a chance. She pressed her foot to the pedal and sped up. The police car was almost on her tail.

"That'll make things worse," she reasoned, taking her foot off of the gas. Flipping her right blinker on, she pressed the brakes and coasted over to the side of the road. When the Corvette came to a complete stop, she reached underneath her seat for the gun.

Watching from her rearview mirror, the officer climbed out of the car. Before advancing toward Nikki, he pulled a walkie-talkie to his lip.

"Oh, God," she cried. Maybe the officer did know. Was he calling for backup?

The closer he approached her car, the tighter she gripped the gun.

He stopped in front of her window and leaned down to get a good look at her face. "Hey there." He grinned, displaying a set of mustard-coated teeth. His breath reeked of cigarettes, coffee, and something dead.

Nikki's smile was innocent. "Hey."

"Reason why I pulled you over is 'cuz you was goin' 'bout a hun-erd back there. And ya know the speed limit's seven-nee."

Nikki closed her eyes with relief. This wasn't about Chance. But she didn't want a ticket, either—a paper trail would not be in her best interest.

Batting her eyes, she smiled seductively at the policeman. "Yes, Officer. Sometimes I don't even realize how fast I'm going in this thing. The ride's so smooth, I can hardly tell." She gave a little laugh.

"Yeah, well. This here's a nice car you got. I'd hate for ya drivin' so fast in it to be the cause of yo' death *or* someone else's, you know what I mean?"

"I understand, Officer. I'll be more careful. Promise."

"I still need to see ya driver's license, registration, and proof of insurance, please."

"Oh, of course." Nikki dropped the gun smoothly and reached for her purse.

He leaned back and waited patiently.

After she handed the cards to him and he walked back to his car, she fumbled with her sweaty fingers. Would he pull something up and take her in? A couple of minutes later, he got out of the car and walked back toward her window. She cursed when she realized she had not picked the gun back up in case. By the time she thought about reaching for it, he was giving her cards back to her.

"All right now. I'm not gon' write you a ticket or nuthin.' You jes' be more careful, aight?"

"Thank you for understanding, Officer."

"No problem. Be safe, okay?"

"Okay." She watched the policeman walk back to his car.

Gripping her chest, she thanked God even though she didn't deserve it. For the rest of the ride she continued to pray, because she certainly was going to need Him again with Duncan.

Chapter Thirty-Two

T he sun floated on top of the horizon; orange and yellow light shooting into the dark blue sky. Driving slowly through her neighborhood, Nikki wondered about Chance's afterlife. Did child molesters have a place in heaven?

Not often did she pray to God or ask Him to forgive her for her sins. Church was a place she rarely visited. Would He still accept her apologies even though she hardly ever reached out to Him? Would His arms be open to her when her time came?

Pulling up in the driveway, she spotted both the Hummer and Mustang through the window of the garage. After turning off the car, she sat there, allowing calmness to set. Easier said than done. The longer she sat, the more worry consumed her. How was Duncan going to react? Glancing at the clock, she decided to climb out of the car. It was almost six.

Opening the front door to the quiet home, she paused. "Dammit!" After the four-hour drive from Vegas, she still didn't know what she was going to tell her husband.

She paced throughout the living room, trying to pull her thoughts together before heading upstairs to the master bedroom.

On the way past Rayshad's bedroom, she opened the door to find her son lying there dreaming peacefully. She loved him so much. He meant everything to her.

Tipping up the hallway, television chatter echoed behind her bedroom door. They never slept with the TV on. Maybe Duncan had fallen asleep. She pushed the door open and almost jumped when she found him lying in the bed wide awake. A remote control was in his hand.

"*You're* home early," he said, without taking his eyes off the infomercial. He lifted the remote and flipped through the channels.

Nikki wasn't sure what he meant by that. "Everything's okay, now. Ma—"

"Before you start lying…" Duncan said, moving a pillow on the bed to unveil his .32.

Nikki twisted her lips, wondering why he had his gun in bed with him.

"I think I should let you know that I called your mother." His gaze locked on her. "She hasn't seen or heard from you for a while now."

Nikki was speechless. She hadn't counted on Duncan calling her mother! What else did he know?

"So, let's start all over again." He focused his attention back on the television. "You're home early," he repeated, his tone as sarcastic as when he'd said it the first time.

"Duncan…" Nikki didn't know what to tell him, and frankly, she was still irritated with him about Marie. She stepped forward. "Baby…" She hadn't called him that in a long time. "I'm going to be honest with you. I had to take care of some business, and right now…right now, I can't tell you."

"A secret?" Duncan said, followed by a bitter laugh that chilled her to the bone. "We're married," he reminded her. "What is there that you *wouldn't* be able to tell me?"

She crossed her arms. "Don't. *You* know more than I do about keeping secrets. So don't even—"

"Oh really? Well, I guess you consider us tit for tat, now?"

Nikki's gaze lowered. "What are you talking about?"

Duncan looked her in the eyes. "I know all about your escapade in Las Vegas."

"What?" Nikki's heart dropped. "I…I…We…I didn't."

Duncan stood up. "Stop it, Nikki! Stop the bullshit. I know all about Chance, okay? *And* this affair you've been having with him this past month. Shit, it's probably been going on longer than that."

Nikki felt walls closing in. If Duncan knew that much about the situation, she was bound to get caught. How did he trace her steps?

"So, what?" He spread his arms out beside him. "You think you've gotten back at me for Marie? Is that it?" He didn't give her time to respond. "That was years ago," he explained, "and I apologized to you so many times, Nikki. Admitted that I was wrong. I promised I would never do anything like that to hurt you, again. I can't believe that you would stoop so low."

"You really don't understand what's been going on," Nikki said.

"Make me understand," he demanded.

Nikki shook her head. "Just know that everything's fine. There's nothing you should be worried about."

Duncan crossed his arms. "Well, I'm not convinced."

Nikki closed her eyes. How could she convince him?

"And really, I can't believe you would do this, after all of the things I've done for you."

"How do you think I felt when I found out about Marie?"

"So, that *is* what this was all about!"

"No—"

"At this point, I don't know what to believe." He stood back up and stepped up to her. "You were probably messing around with him before you even found out about Marie."

"No, I wasn't! I swear! I've done nothing to jeopardize our relationship."

"A trip to Vegas with your ex-husband wouldn't jeopardize our marriage? What kind of business would you have to discuss with him? Wait a minute. That's right. He's an attorney. Was divorce something you might have discussed?"

"I have my business affairs just as you do," she snapped. "And I'm not involved in yours. I didn't do anything you should be worried about. Not like you did with Marie."

"You think I got her pregnant on purpose? Just because you didn't get pregnant during this affair doesn't make your situation any better."

"What I'm saying is: things didn't go as far as you're thinking. You think that I slept with Chance?"

"Hell, you had a hotel room!" Duncan exclaimed.

"Duncan, it was strictly business. That's all you need to know." Nikki could think of nothing else to say to convince him. She was concerned with how she was going to get away with Chance's murder now that Duncan knew that she was the last person with him.

"I'll be in the guest bedroom downstairs," she said, turning to leave.

"I want a divorce," Duncan said as she grabbed the doorknob.

Nikki froze and closed her eyes tightly. "Duncan…"

"You heard me. I want a divorce."

Turning sharply, her lips quivered. "Because of *this?* Nothing happened. I promise you! And, hell, I wasn't trying to divorce you back when Marie had the nerve to step foot on my doorstep."

"That doesn't have anything to do with what's going on right now! If you wanted to divorce me over that, you should've spoken up. But why would you when you have nowhere to go? It's not like you have a job."

"Well, hell, I could get one, but that's not the point."

"Do that then," Duncan said. "Or, better yet, go back to Chance and let him take care of you."

Nikki's eyes flashed fire.

"But even *he* would be a fool to take *your* ass back."

Chapter Thirty-Three

"After all the things I've put up with!" Olivia had read and seen *Waiting to Exhale* too many times. She stormed around the house, gathering all of Chance's belongings into black trash bags. Her mind soared endlessly with ideas as to how she could do damage with each minute that went by and he didn't show up. So far, it had been more than two days.

"How could he do this to me again?" Olivia cried as she remembered busting him a year earlier.

After she had checked his pants pockets, searched through his car, and followed him around, she'd found herself in her sister's car parked outside of a hotel. It took every ounce of will she had to stay in the car while she watched her boyfriend follow a strange woman inside. When they opened the door over an hour later, Olivia stood before them with her arms crossed. "Hello, Chance. Who's your friend?"

But she had forgiven him. He had promised to never cheat again and proposed soon after.

Stuffing another trash bag on the floor of their closet,

she jumped when the doorbell rang. "Who in the—?" she mumbled to herself, dropping two pairs of his shoes. She threw on her robe and made her way downstairs hoping this was not her sister. If it wasn't Chance, she wasn't in the mood to deal with anyone.

She snatched the door open and looked between the two men standing before her. One held up a badge. "Olivia Townsend?"

She looked between the two gentlemen, confused by their presence on her doorstep. She closed her robe tighter, cinching it at her waist. "Yes?"

"We have to ask you to come with us."

Her eyes narrowed. She stood in place with one hand on her hip and the other on the doorframe. "Not before you tell me what's going on."

"Do you know Chance Brown?"

"He's my fiancé," she said.

One detective looked at the other. "A man named Chance Brown was found in a Las Vegas hotel earlier today."

"Found?"

"Dead, ma'am. We're very sorry."

Olivia's eyes bulged out of their sockets and her lips quivered. She covered her mouth and shook her head. "Not *my* Chance." Her eyes filled with tears as she continued to grip her mouth.

"We know it's difficult, but we need you to come down and identify his body."

"Oh! Oh my God! I can't believe this is happening!" She bent over and sobbed.

"I know, Ms. Townsend," said one of the investigators. "We—"

"How? What happened?"

"As of now, it appears he may have possibly overdosed."

"Oh no!" she cried, covering up her entire face. She was aware of his habit, but never thought this would happen.

"There were no wounds or signs of struggle."

"What about his ex-wife? What does she know?"

"As of now, we have no witnesses. Is there something she would know?"

"She was in Vegas with him."

The two men looked at one another. "And how do you know that, ma'am?"

She shook her head. "I know."

"And her name?"

"Nikki. Nikki Johnson."

Chapter Thirty-Four

Nikki scribbled her signature on the receipt and slid it to the dark brown lady in front of her. "It's good seeing you, again, Brenda."

Her ex-co-worker smiled. "You, too. How long are you staying?" she asked, typing something on the computer.

"Maybe a week. I don't know."

Brenda looked at the computer screen and typed all of the information in quickly. "I see you've changed a bit since you used to work here. Lost a little weight, got longer hair." She glanced down at Nikki's fake breasts and added, "You look good."

Nikki smiled. "Thanks."

"How's your son? What's his name again?"

"Rayshad."

"Yeah. How's he doing? Is he in college yet?"

"No. Not yet. Not until next year."

"That's good. I know he's doing good in school. The boy was a little genius back last time I saw him."

"Yeah. My baby's pretty smart. Already has colleges offering him full scholarships."

"That's wonderful. Tell him I said hey. Is he coming through, today?"

"That reminds me." Nikki grabbed her cellular phone. She didn't want him to go home and freak out once he saw that everything was gone. The movers had put everything to storage right after he left for school.

As she was about to dial her son's number, his name popped up and her phone started ringing. "Coincidence," she murmured.

"Hello?"

"Ma."

"Hey, Rayshad." She grabbed her hotel key from Brenda and thanked her before walking off. "I was about to call you."

"Ma, I just got home from school," he whispered. "And there are police cars everywhere."

Nikki felt a swift punch to the gut. "What?"

"Where are you?"

"*What's* going on?" She walked outside as quickly as she could.

"I don't know yet. I just pulled up."

This can't be happening. She had made most of the evidence disappear. There was only one person who could tie her to the crime. And he might have been mad enough to sink her on this one.

"Hello?"

Nikki adjusted the phone. "Yeah, babe. I'm out shopping right now. You said police cars are everywhere? Why?"

"They won't tell me yet. They wanted me to let them know if you called me."

"Okay." She was about to hang up the phone when she heard him call out.

"Ma," he said. "Are you coming home? I think they want to speak with you."

"I'll be there in a minute. Call me once you find out what's going on."

"All right, then."

Nikki disconnected the call and paced back and forth in front of the Beverly Hilton. What was she going to do? Where would she go? She couldn't go back home.

Her phone rang less than sixty seconds later. She pressed a button before her son's call tune could finish.

"Oh my God, Ma."

"What? What is it?"

"Duncan's dead, Ma!"

Nikki slumped against the wall. "What?"

"They're taking his body away, right now."

"Are you serious?"

"Yes, Ma! I'm looking at him—Oh my God! He's really dead!"

She heard a few voices in the background and then he came back on the line.

"And they're taking me in, Ma. They say they want to ask me some questions."

Nikki's heart dropped.

"What am I gonna do, Ma?"

"Don't go," she suggested.

"They want to speak to you, too."

Nikki burst out in tears. "Oh my God." She could hear Rayshad whimpering. "I'll be there in a minute."

But that was a lie, because the moment she hit the expressway, she knew she couldn't go back. Not even for him.

Chapter Thirty-Five

"Ma? Ma, it's me!" She sped through traffic.

"Nikki, are you okay?"

Hitting the brakes, Nikki grabbed her chest as the car in front of her slowed down. "Ma, Duncan's dead!" Swerving into another lane, she accelerated past every car around.

"What?"

Nikki continued sobbing. "And they're coming for me right now, Ma. I know it!"

"Hold on, slow down. *Who's* coming for you?"

"The police, Ma. I know I'm going down for this one. That's why I need you."

"*Me?* Why would you need me?"

Nikki held her breath. "I need you to tell them that I was somewhere else when everything happened. I need you to be my alibi."

Silence.

"Hello?" Nikki looked at the phone to see if the call disconnected. "Are you still there?"

"Yeah," Gina replied helplessly. "I'm still here."

"Are you going to help me, Ma?"

Gina waited a few more seconds before replying, "I'm afraid that I can't."

"What?"

"I can't lie for you, Nikki."

"What? Why not?" A combination of fear and anger continued to rise within her. She would have helped her mother out in a situation like this. But when Nikki thought about the past, she knew why her mother refused. Images of the day she had run away from that horrible scene shot through her mind. Back then Nikki was afraid. She had every reason to be afraid. She was a child! How could her mother hold that against her?

"What am I gonna do, Ma?"

"If you did nothing wrong," Gina replied, "then you should have nothing to worry about."

Before Nikki had a chance to respond, she slammed on her brakes. She prayed she could stop in time as the car's rear end before her loomed into view. Turning the wheel sharply, she swerved the Corvette out of the way but went into a tailspin.

Circling like a dream, everything moved in slow motion. Even though she had her foot smashed on the brakes, there were too many cars around for her to come out safely. Nikki closed her eyes wondering, *Is this the end?*

Rayshad.

Her eyes flew open and the car had not stopped spinning.

Chance. Duncan.

Nikki saw the eighteen-wheeler coming straight for her.

"No!"

The truck crashed into her car, full impact. *BOOM!* And glass shattered everywhere.

Rayshad.

The taste of blood.

Pain.

Darkness.

The sound of screeching metal ripped through Nikki's ears and pulled her out of her sleep. *Was it all a dream?* Peeling her eyes open, the dim light that came into view told her that it wasn't. She pulled herself up from the smelly bed and brushed her orange suit off. A bad taste in her mouth bore a nasty resemblance to the stale odor in her cell.

"Johnson!" a voice echoed.

Nikki looked up. A guard stood at the opening of her cell.

Run, she often thought. *You'll find a way out.* But she stayed frozen to her cot. *One day, though. One day, she would escape.*

"Come with me."

Excitement rushed through Nikki as she stood, wiped the perspiration from her face, and smoothed a hand over her cornrows. She didn't have to glance at the water-stained calendar on the dirty wall to calculate how long it had been. Thirteen long, lonely months of sadness with only four-hundred-sixty-one months and twenty-six more days to go. She never realized how far her mind stretched when there was nothing else to do.

She had written to her mother only to find out that Gina had passed away.

She had sent a few letters to Rayshad, but he only had written back once.

All she wanted was a letter. Surely Rayshad wasn't *that* busy. When she had finally received it, Nikki never thought she felt happier. Ever. Especially when she had found out that he was coming to visit.

Her baby, she thought, pressing the letter up against her chest. The only thing she had left in this world. Nikki had read the letter so many times that she had lost count. It was the only way she could hear his "voice."

Nikki followed the guard to the visitation area. Growing more anxious to see her son, she exhaled and smiled. But when she looked around and couldn't find him, she frowned. There weren't that many people in the place. Where was he?

The guard continued walking, guiding her to the designated booth.

Who was this? She narrowed her eyes, taking a better look. A beautiful, slender woman, with long hair and wearing too much makeup sat before her in a pink dress. The woman leaned back, gracefully crossing one leg over the other and smiled.

That smile! She would know it anywhere.

"Rayshad?"

The woman lowered her lashes and pursed her lips in a seductive manner. "Hey, Ma." He looked Nikki over. "What are you thinking?"

Nikki's eyes watered. Frozen, she stood stiff and emotionless. The world tilted a little to the left and she almost landed on the floor. She closed her eyes to get her bearings. When she opened them, she found this wasn't a dream, either.

Rayshad lowered his head. "I'm sorry," he said, smiling awkwardly. He tried to lighten the mood by spreading his arms wide and offering a little shimmy. "Ta-da!"

Nikki shook her head. Lips tight, she stared at him blankly.

"Now that I've come all the way out, I want the world to see me for who I really am."

Tears flooded her eyes, spilling over as she cried out. Guards, other inmates, and visitors around them turned toward the noise, but she couldn't stop even if she wanted.

"Ma?"

Nikki wiped her nose. "I didn't do what I did for you to end up like this!"

Rayshad's smile melted and he leaned back in the seat. He pursed his lips, glaring at the people who were still staring at them.

Nikki's lips trembled in an effort to say something, but the words wouldn't come.

"Ma, it took me a year—a whole year to get up enough nerve to come see you, and show you how free I feel now."

Nikki couldn't believe what she was hearing. "Free?" He wasn't the one who was in prison, all alone.

"I sat at home all this time thinking about you every day. And I knew that if no one else would accept me… you would, Ma."

Nikki shook her head. "This is *not* what I wanted…" And he knew that. Why was he doing this to her?

"What *you* want? What *you* want?" He threw his hands in the air.

Her eyes landed on his French-tipped acrylic nails.

"Ma, is it always about you? Are you sure that you killed him for me, because I'm thinking it was for you."

"Excuse me?"

"It wasn't for me. I wouldn't have told you to do what you did, because *this* is the last place I would want you to be." His lips trembled. "Ma, you were my best friend, and now, I don't have that anymore. I never should have told you what he did to me. Killing him didn't change anything. Chance is gone, and I'm still the same."

"No. You're not the same. You *were* a man. Now, you're *trying* to be something that you're not."

"This is *me*, Ma. It's who I am. It may not seem right to you, but this is real for me. It's what I want; it's what I love. I feel beautiful. I feel elegant. I feel free!"

An image of Rayshad as a baby flickered through Nikki's mind. Holding him in her arms, she knew he was going to grow up to be a big, strong man.

Looking at the strangely beautiful woman across from

her was another reminder that Chance really deserved his fate.

But, if Nikki had known that Rayshad was going to turn out this way, she would have pled guilty while on trial and explained why she had killed Chance. Maybe she would have received a lighter sentencing. Bad enough, she was also being charged for a death in the car accident prior to her getting arrested.

"I heard about Grandma," Rayshad said.

"Yeah. She told me a while ago that she had cancer. I wish I could have spent more time with her before she left. Or before I got sent away."

"She had cancer?"

Nikki rolled her eyes. Why were they even having this conversation?

"Well, that's not why she died."

She frowned. "It's not?"

"After you went away, she took too much medicine with a whole bunch of liquor."

Tears filled Nikki's eyes. "I can't believe it." Gina had died shortly after her sentencing. Something told her that she had driven her mother to it.

"But hell, that's more believable than what I'm seeing right now!" Nikki wiped her tears. "Do you know Gina would roll over in her grave if she knew that you were a drag queen?"

Rayshad shook his head. "I'm not a drag queen. I am a woman. A woman trapped in a man's body."

"Trapped in a man's body?" Nikki rolled her eyes.

"And do you really think I care about what other people think about me? It's *my* life and I'm gonna live it the way I want to! All of my life, I've had to conform to everyone else's standards and ideals! But what about what I think is best for *me*? I thought that was *my* decision!" Rayshad stopped talking to look at Nikki pathetically. "You don't get it, Ma."

"No, *you* don't get it," Nikki interjected. "You don't understand what's going on in your mind right now. You have no idea. All of this shit that's going on with you right now is something psychological. You need help! You don't even realize that the only reason why you like men now is because of what Chance forced you to do as a child."

"You keep going on and on about Chance when this isn't even about Chance."

"Yes it is."

"See, you've already missed the big picture." Rayshad drew an invisible square in the air. "And it really hurts me that you were mistaken. I hate that things happened the way they did. But then again, I would have never thought that you would have taken such drastic measures, either."

Nikki frowned, searing her son's face for some sign of guilt. "What are you talking about?"

Rayshad looked in another direction and did not answer right away. "Chance never molested me, Ma."

Nikki blinked and replayed his words twice. "What did you just say?"

"Chance never raped me."

Numbness crawled over Nikki as her mouth dropped and her eyes ran wildly over his face. All of her thoughts exploded as she fought the urge to lunge at her son, but she looked at the guard whose gaze swung in her direction and then took deep breaths.

"He used to beat me for little things and talked to me like I meant nothing to him," Rayshad continued, "but after you told me that he wasn't my father, it made sense. It was all you."

Nikki's eyes widened in disbelief.

"He was angry at you for the same reason I was mad with Carissa's ass!"

Nikki pounded the table with her fist. "Then why did you lie?"

"I never lied," he replied. "*You* assumed. You didn't even give me a chance to tell you."

Nikki replayed that day in her mind and couldn't believe she had taken Rayshad's silence as a dead giveaway. "Why didn't you tell me something? Why would you leave me under that impression?" She couldn't stop shaking her head. "This isn't making any sense."

His shoulders slowly elevated. "I don't know. I…" Rayshad's eyes expressed sympathy but his frown told another story. "Does it even matter? I don't care who I told you molested me; I never thought that you were going to go kill him!"

Nikki closed her eyes and took a deep breath. When she opened them and looked into his, she did not know the person sitting before her. She searched her son's expression, noting that he couldn't stop twisting his hands. He looked away nervously and his knee bobbed up and down.

"So are you going to tell me the truth, or are you buying time to come up with a lie?" she asked dryly.

Rayshad inhaled deeply as tears fell from his eyes. He crossed his arms, held his elbows, and began rocking back and forth. "I'm sorry for everything that happened, Mom. I am."

"Then tell me, dammit!"

Through the blue eye shadow, false lashes, and dark eye liner, Nikki found her baby boy's eyes. They were the saddest she had ever seen, but she was unaffected by them. Those were the same eyes he had given her the day he had lied on Chance. The same eyes he used when denying his true sexuality. What stood before her was a lie, because he was not really a woman—not in her eyes.

Rayshad gracefully tossed a pile of long, brown hair off of his shoulders and pursed his trembling lips. "It was Duncan, Ma."

Nikki froze without any emotion. All she could hear was her heart pounding in her chest. With all of her son's secrets and lies, could she even trust Rayshad anymore? An image of Duncan flashed through her mind and like an epiphany slapping her in the face, she fell back in her seat.

"No." She looked at Rayshad, blinked hard, and shook her head. "It couldn't be."

Rayshad began sobbing.

"It was you," she murmured. "It was you all along."

Covering both hands with his face, Rayshad's crying became uncontrollable.

"Why didn't you tell me?" Nikki cried. "Answer me!"

"You wouldn't have handled it any differently than I did, I see," Rayshad said.

That motherfucker! Nikki thought. She couldn't believe that she had taken her son from one abusive stepfather to another. She remembered back when she would wake up in the middle of the night and Duncan wouldn't be in bed. No wonder Rayshad had had problems with his mattress.

"Oh my God," Nikki said, as her head started spinning. "I really think I'm going to be sick."

Nikki wanted to slap herself for not knowing what her own son was capable of. She couldn't believe that he was so selfish that he would allow her to take the blame for a murder that she didn't commit.

But what scared her more than anything was the fact that Rayshad was like her. Chills slid through Nikki's body as she looked at her son, who was almost an exact replica of herself.

"I didn't mean to hurt anybody." He sniffled. "I really didn't. I…I was tired of people always walking all over me. All of my life! I wanted to stand up for myself! For once!"

Nikki's face softened. She tried to allow sympathy to fill her soul, but the reality of the situation sank in. She had been judged more harshly because of Duncan's murder.

"I can't be mad at anyone but myself," Nikki said calmly. "Even though I did that for you. But, I really can't believe that over some straight bullshit, I've lost all the people I've ever loved. My husband, my mother's gone. Chance. And now…" She stopped and shook her head. "And, now, I don't even have a son."

"Don't say that, Ma," he said, wiping away his tears. "You still got me. You've got that daughter you never had." He laughed nervously.

Nikki looked up at him with tight, cold eyes. "I wanted you to make me proud. That's all." She shook her head and swallowed the bad taste in her mouth. "But, I do love you. I *still* love you with all my heart. *That's* why I'm here."

Nikki sped up the highway and watched Los Angeles fade in the rearview mirror through her shades. Her long hair flew in the air like a shiny cape. Looking ahead at the sun setting on the horizon, she exhaled and smiled. No one would know where to find her. She laughed and still couldn't believe that everything went as planned.

After several hours of driving, Nikki arrived in Las Vegas and handed her keys to the valet of the Bellagio.

The tall, dark young man held onto the keys a little bit longer than Nikki had expected. She winked and sashayed away, wondering if he noticed the lump on her neck, which was always a dead giveaway.

When she stepped inside, she pulled a compact mirror out of her clutch and examined her jaw line closely. After several surgeries, she was still not completely satisfied with her appearance. Since she had no intention of ever returning to California, she planned on finding a good plastic surgeon in Vegas—that and a hormone therapist.

She quickly closed the mirror when she saw a glimpse

of her mother in the reflection. Nikki had her regrets, but if she could do it all over again, she wouldn't have done a thing differently. The money she had received from Chance's insurance policy and Duncan's estate was a lot more than she had expected, affording her the life-altering surgery she always had desired.

After checking in, she started unpacking her dresses while contemplating her next move.

A small black spider crawling up the wall caught her attention. Quickly grabbing a cup on the bathroom sink, she captured the creature, opened the window, and let him free. Fresh air flowed through as she inhaled and took in the amazing view. The city glittered with colorful lights beneath the cloudy sky, gifting her with the opportunity to fulfill her next dream of becoming a star.

She turned to look in the full-sized mirror across the room and picked up the last dress she had unpacked. Holding the purple gown against her frame, she considered wearing it out that night. She had no set plans, but knew she wanted to enjoy the nightlife. Maybe the valet could point her in the right direction.

Nikki placed the dress across the bed and finished unpacking. When she pulled a photo of her mother out of the luggage, she froze and a tear dropped from her eye. The gorgeous lady with red lips struck a pose while blowing a kiss. She tried not to think about the last time seeing her. That orange suit. Her cornrows. Heartache and tears. Never had she seen her mother so disappointed.

After her mother had committed suicide by hanging, Nikki had made a vow that she would live forever through her. She tucked the photo on the vanity mirror, then blew a kiss back.

Several other items she unpacked went without notice until she came across a wrinkled newspaper clipping with a picture of Carissa. The article detailed the recovered body of a young mother that had been missing for months. Nikki questioned why she was still holding on to the yellowing paper and crumpled it into a ball.

After a long shower, she slid into the purple dress and pushed her big breasts in place. Looking into the full-length mirror, she stood tall and confident and smiled. Such a replica of her mother that it scared her sometimes. Almond eyes; soft, round nose; and pink plump lips.

An image of her before the operation crossed her mind and she remembered how uncomfortable she was dressing as a female. But now that she really was a woman, nothing could hold her back from doing all she could to make the world fall in love with her.

Taking a seat before the vanity, she picked up a makeup brush. After carefully crafting her face, she raised a perfectly arched eyebrow high above her shimmery eyes and puckered her shiny, pink lips. Indeed she had learned from the best.

From behind her, a sharp, cold breeze pressed through the open window. The curtains fluttered softly as the smell of a storm brewing invaded the small room. Against the gray sky, the colorful lights brought about the perfect balance. She loved when it rained and wouldn't dare to let it interfere with her night.

As she stood, winds grew stronger and whistled an ugly tune. Thunder boomed and lightning slashed through the dark gray clouds. But before one raindrop made its way inside, with one push, Nikki slammed the window shut.

About the Author

E.V. Adams is a Journalism major and freelance writer, currently residing in Jackson, MS. She can be found on FaceBook or reached via email: evadams777@yahoo.com.

ARE YOU CURIOUS ABOUT THE NALEIGHNA KAI NOVEL
CARISSA AND NIKKI ENJOYED? WHET YOUR APPETITE
FOR A GOOD READ WITH THIS EXCERPT FROM

Every WOMAN Needs A Wife

BY NALEIGHNA KAI
AVAILABLE FROM STREBOR BOOKS

CHAPTER One

"I could kill both of you," she said softly. "I'd probably go to jail, but I certainly won't feel guilty…"

Brandi Spencer turned the key in the ignition, still trying to come up with a good opening line as she braced herself to walk in on her husband and his mistress. Killing them would be too quick and painless. She wanted them to suffer.

Settling into the black leather seat, she tried something

else. "Heifer, what the hell do you think you're doing with my husband?" No, too common and too weak. She'd have to use something a bit stronger than *heifer*.

"Vernon, do you think I'm stupid? Did you think I wouldn't find out?" That was lame and overused. She had let this thing ride for six months before deciding to confront him.

"Since I'm paying for half of this affair, what's in it for me?"

That might work!

Fingers of doubt sent a chill through her; she knew Vernon would have every excuse in the book.

The fading sunlight cast a subdued glow into the car. Leaning back in the cool seat, she realized that asking for a divorce while the woman he'd been sneaking around with for the past six months was looking on wouldn't leave him any breathing room. And she didn't mind one bit if he choked on what she was about to serve up. *If* she could find the courage. She reached into her purse, grabbed her equipment, and placed it in her bra, tucking it out of sight.

Brown and yellow leaves danced in the chilly October wind as Brandi left the security of her car and inched her way toward what could be a total liberation or her worst nightmare. Doing the unthinkable tugged at her mind, but common sense kicked in. How long would the pleasure from killing them last? She had to find a better way.

Walking up the cobblestone path, she gazed at the house

her accountant said Vernon had paid for out of their business account. Taking a long, slow breath, she knocked on the wooden door.

Moments later, a tall, blonde with deep-set blue eyes and a curvaceous figure some women would give an ovary to have, appeared in the doorway. She was wearing a sheer red robe and not much else.

Gathering her strength, Brandi abandoned her rehearsed lines. "Good evening, Tanya. I'd like to speak with you and my husband," she said, breezing past the mistress into a spacious, tastefully furnished living room.

"Husband? Wait a minute," the woman shrieked, grabbing for Brandi, who shimmied just out of reach. "You must have the wrong house. Your husband's not here."

"Oh, yes he is," Brandi shot back, outrage fast replacing fear as she stood facing Vernon—a man whose charisma, handsome face, and tall, muscular build had put moisture in the driest panties. "That man right there on your sofa is actually married…to me." Brandi flashed her wedding ring in the woman's face before venturing further into the room. The table had been set with a candlelight dinner for two. The scent of grilled steak, mashed potatoes, and apple cobbler mingled with the fresh citrus smell of the house. Somehow, Brandi didn't think that the cozy little dinner would grace Tanya's lips—or Vernon's.

A quick glance at the mistress showed a flash of pink coloring the woman's high cheekbones before her sensuous red lips tightened into a hard line. She was strikingly pretty, with a heart-shaped face and classically pert nose. She looked as though she belonged on the pages of *Cosmo* or *Vogue* rather than hidden away in a bungalow on the south side of Chicago.

Vernon, dressed in a casual suit that complemented his warm brown skin, short-cropped hair, and piercing dark brown eyes, had been lounging comfortably on a plush maroon sofa in the living room when Brandi stormed in. He had one leg thrown over the arm, a glass of cognac in one hand and a remote control in the other. He quickly switched off the television, leaving only the faint sound of music drifting in from the dining room. His eyes widened to the size of saucers and his thin mustache twitched just before his jaw dropped. He jumped up, spilling the warm amber liquid onto the cream carpet. His mouth opened and closed, opened and closed, looking like a fish waiting for the first available hook. The action seemed to swallow every other sound in the room.

Unable to conceal a satisfied smile, Brandi used the calmest voice she could manage. "I want her to come live with us."

This time, Tanya's jaw dropped. Her face went from slightly tan to white as chalk in mere seconds. But the mistress recovered a lot faster than Vernon, whose mouth still hadn't closed. Brandi's lips lengthened into something between a sneer and a smirk.

"We're going to end the deception you've got going and save some money, too. As your wife, and the person who's footing the bill for this affair, I don't think this is an unreasonable request." Brandi leaned in close enough to catch a whiff of his earthy cologne. "The nerve of you to charge her upkeep to the business. You *wanted* to get caught."

"Baby, I'm just waiting on Jeremy and Craig, I—"

Brandi put up a single hand before whirling to face the woman who had entered her marriage like a bad odor on a windy day. Tanya stared back at her as though she had lost her mind. Brandi was beginning to question her own sanity, but watching her oh-so-handsome husband lose his cool had its own rewards.

Finally, Vernon backed slowly away, almost stumbling over the glass end table, putting some distance between him and his pissed-off wife. "You've got a lot of balls showing up here."

"That's right," Brandi shot back keeping in step with him. "I have my own pair, and right now I'm holding yours, too, my brother."

"Where are the girls?" he demanded, finally getting his bearings.

Tanya's shock finally gave way to anger as she folded her slender arms across her full breasts, glaring at Vernon. "Wife? You, you didn't say anything about a *living* wife! You said she died in childbirth and—"

The rush of words came to an abrupt halt as Brandi interrupted, with a bitter chuckle, "Yeah, right about now I think he wishes that was true."

The temperature in the room rose ten degrees. Brandi smiled sweetly, watching Vernon creep away and slump back onto the sofa. His eyes darted around the room as he grimaced, mumbling something she couldn't quite catch.

"Mr. Smooth himself, speechless? Definitely a first," Brandi taunted, following him, then leaning in, lowering her voice to a breathy whisper. "But what can you say, *Mr.* Spencer? The marriage license is burning a hole in my purse as we speak." She grinned. "I'd like to see you work a lie around this one." And the man could tell them, too. He could lie well enough to make a hooker pay premium price for what she got free every day. Brandi had fallen for a few lines in her lifetime, sweeping the smallest ones to the side to keep peace in her home. Those days were over.

Vernon slowly stood to his full height of six foot two and glared down at his wife. "I don't know what you're talking about. Check the record, Brandi. She's a client."

"Bullshit!" she snapped, head whipping around to the mistress. "A client? A *white* one at that?" Brandi lowered her gaze to the woman's groin. "Wearing a robe so sheer I can see blonde hairs covering the gateway to heaven. Or should I say the gateway to hell, if she doesn't know what to do with it."

Tanya wrapped the robe closer, averting her eyes.

"And since I've had to be awful friendly with Mr. Dildo these past six months, she apparently knows how to get you over here." Calm was returning slowly to Brandi. "If I have to use equipment to fulfill my basic needs, and

I'm helping to run the business, taking care of the house, bringing home the bacon, frying it, and cleaning up right after, what the hell do I need you for?"

Vernon's gaze flicked between the two women before settling on Brandi. "She's *only* a client, Brandi," he said, trying to use a convincing tone—a tone that worked with their customers, but not with Brandi. Not anymore.

"You called me a client?" Tanya's words, almost a resigned whisper, had savage simplicity. "A client? You asshole!" She pushed him back onto the sofa with a single hand, strolled to the bar, and poured herself a drink. Brandi almost joined her; she needed a damn stiff drink herself.

All three silently held their ground, each waiting for the other to make the next move.

Tanya's statements only proved what Brandi thought— he'd spent so much time with the woman that she hadn't suspected a thing. Brandi decided she'd delivered her opening lines just right. Now all she had to do was wait for Vernon to tighten the noose around his own neck. Arrogance could always do that to a man, and Vernon had arrogance by the bucketful.

Faint light crept through the vertical blinds and splayed onto the carpet as the icy silence created a sliver of uneasiness that only heightened the tension.

Vernon stood, rubbing his temples. "We'll talk about this when we get home."

"No, we'll talk about this right now," Brandi shot back.

"Vernon," Tanya began, "I think she's right—"

"Shut up," he growled, casting an angry glance at Tanya,

whose alabaster skin blushed once again as he snapped, "You stay out of this!"

"Don't tell me to shut up," she replied evenly, soft curls billowing out around her shoulders. "You brought this into my living room and you've lied to me. I have every right to speak my mind." The woman squared her shoulders, somehow growing her own pair of balls. The change was so subtle, it was neither movement nor sound.

The mistress was a startling contrast to Brandi's honey brown skin, light brown eyes, wide, fleshy hips, and full breasts that always used to make Vernon's mouth water every time he looked at them. Suddenly, Brandi felt a bit self-conscious about those extra fifty pounds. But then, her full-figured frame had never mattered to him—only her leading role in the business they started ten years ago had bothered him, causing more fights than she cared to count.

"Enough of this. This is not going to happen right now," Vernon said, with a swipe of his hand. "Brandi, go home!"

"Technically, I *am* home." Brandi dropped down on the sofa next to her husband, casually crossing one leg over the other. "Thanks to your stupidity, I own part of this one, too." Then a sudden thought came to her. "Hey! You want me and the girls to pack our stuff and move in?" she asked, lifting a single eyebrow as though warming up to the idea. "It'll be a little tight, but then again you're used to tight places." She glanced slyly at Tanya. "But then again, maybe not…"

Anger flashed in the woman's eyes as she cast a narrowed gaze at Brandi, but when she spoke, it was to Vernon. "Deal with this! I can't believe you pulled this crap on me!"

Glancing down, Brandi's anger came back faster than she could rein it in. Tanya had a block of ice on her left hand large enough for a whole village to skate on—with or without lessons.

Tanya edged away from the not-so-happy couple. "You could've gotten me killed. Suppose she came here with a gun?"

"Actually, I don't use those," Brandi said, plucking an imaginary piece of lint from her navy pants. "But I *did* bring a knife. I got it from my friendly neighborhood hoodlums. They say it works a hell of a lot better than a gun. Less chance of discovery. Notice, I haven't touched anything since I've been here."

Tanya's eyes widened as she swallowed hard. "Are you serious?"

Brandi shrugged. "The way I figure it, Biblically I have the right to kill both of you. You know, the adultery and casting the first stone thing and all." She sighed wearily, placing a single hand on her chest. "But stones can be a little messy…"

Tanya glared at her, countering with, "But there is that *do not kill* line in there, too. You do *know* the Ten Commandments, don't you?"

No this heifer didn't come back with that! Brandi leveled

a stony gaze at Tanya, pissed that she had said anything at all, but then grinned anyway and answered, "Yes, Tanya, they're in Exodus. But two books later in Deuteronomy it says that stoning the adulterers is A-okay." She winked. "Now I'm down with that program. You first, babe."

Vernon's look was fierce, almost malicious. "You're out of your mind!"

"No, stud, you're out of yours," Brandi shot back. "How the hell did you think you were gonna keep giving me the short end of the stick?" She lowered her gaze to his waist. "Literally—and think I wouldn't figure it out?" She laughed. The outburst seemed to startle them both. "Normally, I can't get my panties off quick enough. Now I can't get a drive-by sniffing of dick. It doesn't take a master's to realize someone else is getting it, 'cause it certainly isn't me."

Vernon winced, glancing over his shoulder at the now-cold dinner, then into the corner, then slowly back at Brandi. Her gaze followed his, landing on the black briefcase she had given him for their last anniversary. He squinted, speaking through clenched teeth. "You've got things all wrong."

Brandi folded her arms across her breasts. "Oh, really? There's no problem here. I figure if you're gonna sleep with the woman, don't sneak around; just let me in on it." She grinned, hiding the pain that shot through her heart. "I should at least get something out of it. If she's reaping the fruits of my labor, she can come on home with me, help clean the house, wash your dirty drawers, and keep the kids."

Brandi glanced at Tanya, who stared ahead blankly, her bottom lip held prisoner by perfect white teeth. "She can even put some money on the bills, too. I don't have a problem with that. I'm all for *us* having a mistress as long as she does her share of the work. There has to be more to it than her just lying on her back to keep you happy. Hell, I wanna be happy, too. Clean my damn house, help a sister out—take some of the pressure off me."

Tanya flinched as Brandi's words chipped away at her dignity. She resembled a mannequin, staring at Vernon.

Brandi turned to gaze solidly into his face. Her fingertips smoothed over the soft material covering his muscular chest. She straightened the tie loosely draped around his neck. "If you're going to have a mistress—and this marriage is all about sharing, honey—then I should have a mistress, too. Every woman needs a wife."

Turning slowly to face a now-trembling mistress, whose eyes flashed with a glimmer of something that might have been pain, Brandi said, "Tanya, if you're going to sleep with him, you need to earn it just like I do." Then she rose, covering the distance between Tanya and her. A new, shocking idea forming with each step. "And you know what? Since I pay most of the bills, and I'm part of the reason he looks good enough to make you want to spread your legs," she said, swallowing her revulsion as she reached out to cup Tanya's buttocks strictly for effect, "then I'd like some ass, too."

CHAPTER *Two*

T anya's face froze. Surely she hadn't heard right. Emphasizing the point, Brandi stroked Tanya's buttocks with one hand, relishing the woman's wide eyes and tense body with every move. Violated, Tanya's cheeks went from a bright red to white and back.

Brandi leaned in, whispering, "You should know that I'm the real source of the money. So I'm not above you doing me, either."

Tanya trembled, face darkening with anger as she jerked back. She glanced at Vernon and just as suddenly her expression changed. The startled look in her eyes slowly fading, Tanya tilted her head back and roared with laughter.

Interesting, Brandi thought, *and I was only joking.* The request was pure boldness, a way to shock them and frighten the hell out of Vernon. Judging from the third serving of cognac sloshing into his glass, she had managed—but then again, she had more up her sleeve. *If* she could make it home before he did.

Vernon stormed across the living room until the two of them stood eye to eye. "I think you're taking a little too much credit here." He took another long swig of cognac, nearly emptying the glass. "*I'm* the reason we're so successful. It was *my* money that started things. I'm the real reason we made it, so get off it, *Mrs. High and Mighty.*"

Brandi glowered at him. "You mean the money you got from your *daddy?* That was barely lunch money, just enough to buy a refrigerator and stove. And it may have helped to get things off the ground, but the ideas and drive to pull everything together came from me." Her gaze traveled the length of his well-toned body—one that hadn't been draped in anything less than designer suits for years. "The business, the Armani suits, the six-figure income were all a *joint* effort," she said, feeling a sudden rush of anger that he would belittle her efforts. "If I'd left things up to you, we'd still be stuck in that tiny storefront on Michigan Avenue, barely making ends meet. Seems like you forgot all that."

"Wait a minute—"

"Oh, shut up, Vernon!" Brandi dropped back down on the sofa, resting a hand on the arm. Tanya offered her a glass of vodka. Brandi gazed into the woman's eyes for a moment before accepting and taking a sip.

"Either we share Tanya and she helps me around the house, or we divorce right now. You'll keep the mistress," she said, holding up a single finger. "And I'll keep the house, the cars, and get alimony and child support We'll split any profits from The Perfect Fit down the middle. I'm sure she,"—Brandi nodded in Tanya's direction—"won't be happy with what you'll have left. And that will be…" Brandi rubbed her chin, gazing toward the ceiling as though checking an imaginary calculator. "Oh, let me see—about one-fourth of what you make now." She shrugged, grinning at Tanya. "Unless one-fourth will be all right with you?"

Scanning the woman's body, taking in the expensive La Perla dressing gown, remembering the burgundy Lexus sitting in the driveway, the Oriental artwork and Lalique figurines decorating the house, Brandi felt her anger springing forth like molten lava from a volcano. Hell, Brandi didn't drive a damn Lexus! And she'd never purchased anything from Lalique.

As her eyes continued their travel, the engagement ring made her pause—again. The damned thing was twice the size of the one he'd given her for their tenth anniversary, and four times the size of the one he'd given her on their wedding day.

Tanya followed Brandi's gaze to her slender fingers gripping the back of the loveseat. She looked into Brandi's eyes. "I'm truly sorry. I didn't know. Even the girls never mentioned you."

Vernon's eyes widened bigger than golf balls. He glared at Tanya as his lips formed a hard line.

There was no mistaking the sincerity behind the woman's words. Girls? The woman knew her children, too? Vernon would fry!

Tanya glanced at the ring; then at Vernon, whose dark, liquid eyes had filled with worry; and finally to Brandi once again. "He said he was a widower and waited so long to get married again because of his daughters. He wanted to build a business first. Then he told me he wanted his girls to be a little older." She grimaced as a tear fell from her bright eyes. "I wonder what excuse he would've given me next time."

Brandi wasn't a bit surprised; he'd taken this lying thing to a higher level. And now the children, this woman, and Brandi would all feel the crunch. Vernon, ever the man to land on his feet, wouldn't feel a damn thing. She would have to change all that.

Tanya loosened her grip on the soft cushions, pacing angrily, her eyes glazing over with unshed tears. "Amazing what they think they can get away with," she said. Eyes narrowing at him, she snatched off the ring and raised it above her head, aiming to hurl it across the room.

Then she paused, wincing as though struck by lightning, to roll the jewel between her fingers. The diamond was illuminated with a surreal glow, as though it was on display at Tiffany's. The woman's bright smile lit up the room as she faced Brandi, holding up the ring. "You don't mind if I keep this as his going-away present, do you?"

The woman was a lot smarter than she looked. Brandi shrugged, taking a small sip of vodka. "Go right ahead."

Vernon finally found the will to move. His gaze first fell on Tanya, then on Brandi, obviously trying to decide which was the better bargain. After several agonizing moments, he reached for Brandi's hand. "Baby, it's not what you think. She doesn't mean anything to me…"

Brandi's level gaze said she wasn't falling for the bullshit.

"We'll get counseling or something. You can't divorce me…"

Brandi watched the mistress back away, gripping her stomach as though she had been punched. For a split second, Brandi felt a tinge of compassion. She quickly brushed it aside the moment she lowered her eyes to her handsome husband, who had all but sunk to his knees as he put a vise grip around her waist.

He repulsed her, but she didn't pull away from him. She sank down on the sofa once again, listening to his sad speech, letting him say everything he wanted about staying together, that his little fling didn't mean anything—really. Brandi looked up at Tanya, who now stared at Vernon with a faint, bitter smile on her lips as her breasts heaved, a single hand resting on her chest. Tears streamed, pooling at her chin before dripping to the carpet in a steady rhythm. The woman was telling the truth. She hadn't known.

"I can't believe this," Tanya said, staring at the ring, then at Vernon.

Diamonds were truly a girl's best friend, and the size of the one on the woman's finger told Brandi that Tanya was more than just a fling. He was serious, but not serious enough to pull away from the business or his current life. Too late! Brandi would have that all wrapped up, as well as a few other things.

Brandi blinked to clear her vision as Tanya's pain triggered her own. How many nights had she longed for her husband? How long had she allowed the fear of losing him to cloud her judgment?

Tanya wiped her face with the back of a trembling hand, looking more like a child than the beautiful, confident woman who greeted Brandi at the door.

Brandi reached out, stroking Vernon's head gently as he pressed his face into the soft curve of her neck. "Brandi, I can make this up to you. I promise."

She touched him, knowing it would probably be her last time. Her world had changed. It had been easy to imagine the other woman, but seeing her husband in Tanya's house, settled in as though he didn't have a family somewhere else, brought forth emotions no amount of waiting could prepare her for.

While Vernon rattled on, Tanya scurried from the living room. She returned with suitcases, garment bags, all Vernon's things, which she piled directly outside the front door. Brandi watched every move, thinking, *Did she forget that technically this is not her house?* It didn't really matter—right now she was making a statement. Two women, both hurt—one man, the source of the pain. Vernon had lost both of them.

Brandi managed not to laugh as she pushed her husband away. She strolled toward the door, leaving a disgruntled Vernon struggling to get off the sofa to catch up with her. Tanya glanced at her as she touched the knob, their gazes locked in woman-to-woman understanding. If Brandi knew her husband as well as she thought, the rest of the night would prove to be very interesting...